DELIGHTFUL
DISCIPLINE

DELIGHTFUL DISCIPLINE

Humorous Stories
of Woodshed Wisdom
and Biblical Principles

LOUIS R. GOODGAME

BOX 236, MILFORD, MI. 48042

Manufactured in the United States of America

Library of Congress Cataloging in Publication Data

Goodgame, Louis R   1927-
  Delightful discipline.

  1. Conduct of life. 2. Self-control. I. Title.
BJ1581.2.G58   649'.1   77-22560
ISBN 0-915134-43-8

Cover by Wayne Stayskal, Rod Burke Associates

TO

My grandfather, Martin Sadowski,
and his wife Martha—"Pat" and "Busha"—
who raised us strict and straight;

My father, Pete Hooper,
who taught me that a stepfather can love a boy
as his very own,
who took time to be a real friend,
who taught me to shave with a straightedge razor

My dear, sweet Polish mother,
from whom I learned my first and ultimate lessons
in love and firmness.

ACKNOWLEDGMENTS

Jerusalem Bible, ed. Alexander Jones. Doubleday and Co., Inc., 1975.

LB = The Living Bible, Paraphrased. Tyndale House, 1971.

NASB = New American Standard Bible. Moody Press, 1972.

NEB = The New English Bible. Oxford and Cambridge University Presses, 1970.

Phillips = The New Testament in Modern English, trans. by J. B. Phillips. The MacMillan Co., 1958.

CONTENTS

INTRODUCTION

"Goodgame!" the doctor groaned, "find those kids!"

"Find the kids," I muttered in my mind as I raced out the door, "after they've had a two hour head start?"

I was an orderly in a state hospital for emotionally disturbed children. Since this was a new institution, in the experimental stage, policies and practices were constantly changing. The good doctors had just adopted a "permissive program"—no restrictions were to be used. We were cautioned that even if a child ran away, no attempt was to be made to prevent his escape or to give chase. Most of the staff grumbled over such rules, but we were paid to obey.

The children were quick to sense this new atmosphere of unrestrained liberty and promptly took full advantage of their rights. "Childonic" chaos erupted! Most of the staff were wise enough to retreat to the safety of the observation room where accurate reports of the children's behavior could be written. When several of the older boys headed for the hills, we cheerfully waved goodbye. With the ringleaders gone, the rest of the children soon ran out of devilment, and things returned to normal.

The doctors warmly approved our lack of action and predicted that the runaways would soon return.

"They'll soon tire of not being the center of activity," stated the head doctor.

"When they get hungry, they'll come back," added the second in command.

But when several hours had expired and the boys had not returned, the head doctor had a change of philosophy. Perhaps the dread of lawsuits by the parents, some of whom were rather prominent people in Washington, D.C., hastened his decision. He ordered an immediate search by all available staff. Doctors and nurses by cars, teachers by bikes, and poor orderlies by foot. I learned that as in the military, so also in medicine, R.H.I.P. (Rank Has Its Privileges).

I raced in the general direction of where the boys were last seen, cresting a hill. Below lay a wide expanse of escape routes. Other orderlies joined me and plunged on in blind pursuit. I caught my breath, and viewed the possible routes. Would they take the river, or perhaps the highway where they could hitch a ride? Then my eyes caught the glisten of shining rails. I called up boyhood memories and quickly decided that those bright rails were just too irresistible for itchy feet. I felt that boyish urge to "walk the rails" again.

I had to go through some thick brush to reach the tracks, but once on the rails the going was fast. I was walking a rail, balancing myself with outstretched arms, when I found the boys. To be more precise, the boys first saw me, and greeted me with chunks of coal from their coal bin fortress.

"Goodgame!" shrieked Bobby, their leader, "come and get us!"

I squatted down to size up the situation. The boys were on the top of a coal bin with an ample supply of anthracite. Their first volley had fallen some fifty feet short, so I was probably safely out of range. That this was a true rebellion and not a prank was clearly indicated when Bobby called me "Goodgame" instead of "Mr. Goodgame." A frontal attack seemed unwise, neither did I wish to engage in a coal throwing contest. I decided to starve them out.

"Weak arm!" I yelled back. "The girls throw better than that."

The insult drove them to a frenzy. Broadside after broadside belched forth from their fortress. Naturally, I cheered them on. By wasting their pent-up energy, I was increasing their hunger pains and making them easier to handle when I finally got my hands on them.

After some fifteen minutes of rapid fire, the last volley fell limply. A thin, hoarse voice wailed, "Goodgame, have you had enough?"

Flipping off my white jacket, I waved it frantically over my head, and shouted, "I give up! Please, no more coal!"

With roars of laughter the boys scampered down from their castle to claim me as a spoil of war. Duty and honor required that I shake hands with each grimy and grinning conqueror. I respectfully accepted their condolences as they did my congratulations. During these ceremonies, my hospital whites became prison grays.

"Goodgame," Bobby announced, "you're our prisoner, and we're not going back to the hospital."

"We're not?" I gasped in feigned horror. "Then where are you taking me?"

"To Baltimore!" Henry proclaimed.

"But just until we find a boat to Africa," Bobby corrected. "We're going to live in the jungle and hunt elephants."

"Africa!" I gasped. "There are snakes in the jungle." I added this in the hopes it might slow down their thirst to go on safari. Actually, I was happy to be their hostage, for now I could keep an eye on them until the authorities arrived.

"Only girls are afraid of snakes," Bobby spoke for his troops.

"But Bobby," I complained, "Baltimore's a good thirty miles away, and I'm tired and hungry. I want some food!"

The mere mention of food had a dramatic effect as hunger pains asserted themselves and wiped out the ecstasy of victory. Bobby now learned what Napoleon meant when he said that an army "travels on its stomach."

"I'm hungry!" wailed John.

"I am too!" chorused the famished troops.

I sensed an opportunity and pressed into it. "Just my luck to get caught," I grumbled. "By now the other orderlies are returning for dinner."

Bobby just grunted, as the others listened in dismay.

"You know what really grabs me?" I griped as I clutched my stomach for emphasis. "Those doctors and nurses are going to be eating our food, since we won't be there. All those extra hamburgers—"

"Hamburgers!" yelled the boys in unison.

"Yeah, hamburrrgers!" I stretched out the sound. "I can see them now, nestled between white buns, covered with golden mustard, with slivers of pickles—"

"Knock it off!" Bobby ordered. "You won't trick us into returning, not even for hamburgers!"

I noticed that some of his soldiers did not share the same convictions. "Bobby, there's no way I can trick you," I insisted, "because there's just no way we could get those burgers even if we did return."

"What!" yelped John. "They won't feed us if we go back?"

"Just bread and water," Bobby answered. "That's all we'll get, so we ain't going back for that!"

"No," I disagreed, "they'd be glad to see us back, and they'd feed us too. Trouble is, we'd only get leftovers."

"Leftovers!" cried Henry. "Why leftovers?"

"Because by the time we'd get back," I explained, "all the good food would have been eaten. And you know what they'll eat first."

"Hamburgers!" wailed my wandering waifs.

The iron was hot, and I gambled on a final blow. I looked at my watch. "Let's see," I mused, "dinner's in forty-five minutes. It took me an hour to find you; course I wasn't running all the time." They listened in respectful silence.

"Lousy luck!" I growled. "If I wasn't a prisoner, I could make it. Instead I'm chained to a bunch of boys who can't run."

It was an open insult, and Bobby wasn't about to pass it by. "We can run faster than you!" he shouted. "You're nothing but an old man!"

"Then it's a race?" I challenged.

"On one condition," Bobby insisted.

"What's that?" I asked.

"When we beat you back, you've got to admit to the doctors that you didn't catch us—we caught you!"

"Do I have to?" I begged for mercy.

"Yes!" the little monsters roared in happiness.

"Well, at least I won't be the last one back!" I yelled my challenge and tore down the tracks. "Last one back's a nurse!"

With a howl the pack was on my trail as we

raced to save the hamburgers for a better fate. I took a shortcut for the nearest highway, in hopes that the police would spot us and relieve me of my charges.

As I had hoped, we were spotted by one of the doctors. He made a frantic U–turn. I'm certain he must have thought that the boys were howling after me with murder in mind. His car screeched to a stop in front of us, and he leaped out for the rescue. To his shock, the boys piled in and demanded to be taken back to the hospital.

"Goodgame," he whispered as we walked to the car, "why were they chasing you?"

"It's a long story," I hissed, almost out of breath, and then collapsed on the front seat.

"Mr. Goodgame," Bobby said with a new tone of respect in his voice, "you run pretty good for an old man."

"Only when I'm hungry for hamburgers," I wheezed, hoping that my endeavors would not result in a heart attack at the ripe age of thirty-one.

We arrived, and the boys were hustled off to the showers to remove all traces of coal bin. The head doctor held onto me, demanding a full report of what, when, how, and why. I could see he was impressed by my primitive psychology.

"Hamburgers," he sniffed. "You trapped them with hamburgers."

"Yes, sir," I replied, "and if they don't get some, they'll run off again."

He picked up the phone and talked with the cook. The conversation became heated.

"What do you mean we don't have any hamburger?" he roared. "A three million dollar institution, and you tell me we don't have hamburger!"

I couldn't quite catch the cook's excuse.

"Well, what do you have!" he demanded. The

cook gave an inventory of her meat locker. "I don't care if it is sirloin," the doctor snapped. "Grind it up!"

I washed and joined my boys in the dining room. Since the hour was late, we had it all to ourselves. The sirloin hamburgers were positively scrumptious! The cook was hard pressed to keep the burgers rolling. For dessert, we had a choice of cherry pie or chocolate ice cream. We ate both.

After this bout with gluttony, the boys were interested only in bed. They were all asleep before the pillows turned warm.

It was long after quitting time when I left the boys and prepared to go home. The head doctor was waiting for me at the office, and he walked me to the front door. He placed a fatherly arm about me and said, "I'm sure glad you didn't tempt them with hot dogs."

"Oh?" I asked.

"I'd never have talked the cook into making hot dogs out of sirloin!" We both laughed.

"Well, Goodgame," he spoke with a hint of praise, "you did get the kids back."

And that's what this book is all about—discipline practices that work with kids because they are based on common sense and God's Word.

Discipline Principles

Effective discipline requires a basic understanding of children: how they think, act, react, and what is important to them. To understand children, you must be able to think their thoughts and sense their values. Never belittle a child's mind, for the thoughts of children are long and beautiful.

Jesus said it simply and sweetly:

And when the chief priests and scribes saw the wonderful things that he did, and the children crying in the temple, and saying, Hosanna to the son of David; they were sore displeased, and said unto him, Hearest thou what these say? And Jesus saith unto them, Yea; have ye never read, Out of the mouth of babes and sucklings thou has perfected praise? *(Matthew 21:15, 16).*

Discipline Practices

Think of your own childhood. As you recall forgotten events new ones will flash into view. Try to recall the things you liked and disliked as a child. What kind of adult did you like to be around? What things were important to you?

Read books written especially for children. The local librarian is a good source to find out the books children are reading and which ones they enjoy. What children read on their free time gives insight into their thinking and values.

Read books about children. Mark Twain has given some concepts to ponder over in his "Tom Sawyer" and "Huckleberry Finn" classics. I suspect that Samuel Clemens never forgot what it means to be a boy, and that's why he could write so intimately about childhood.

Read books by experts on children, for they have much to say, and usually persist in saying it. A word of caution is in order. You will discover that professionals disagree among themselves. In fact, if carefully read, most disagree with their own words on some issues. So learn all you can from their insights, but hold fast to your common sense.

Talk to adults that children like to be around. There must be a reason why children are attracted to certain old people.

Take time to be with and among children under various experiences, both bitter and sweet. Children are more than playthings. Work with them, study with them, eat with them, think with them, and learn to live with them.

Finally, I would be remiss if I failed to direct you to the greatest Teacher and Disciplinarian the world has even known, Jesus Christ, God's Son. A study of His methods as recorded in the Bible will insure lasting and loving success. How did Jesus win the children? One author has suggested the following methods which He used:

> Jesus was ever a lover of children. He accepted their childish sympathy and their open, unaffected love. The grateful praise from their pure lips was music in His ears, and refreshed His spirit when oppressed by contact with crafty and hypocritical men. Wherever the Saviour went, the benignity of His countenance, and His gentle, kindly manner won the love and confidence of children. (Ellen G. White, *Desire of Ages*, p. 511).

Discipline Proverbs

- It is easier for an adult to think and act like a child, having been one, than for a child to think and act like an adult.

- A wise parent knows how to think like a child but act like an adult.

- We can be forgiven for growing old, but there is no excuse for those who forget their childhood.

And that illustrates the format of the book: **a true story** based on a childhood experience which taught me something about discipline, followed by **Discipline Principles, Practices, Proverbs.**

My purpose in writing this book is to present discipline in an atmosphere of delight and pleasure. Life, even at its worst, should be enjoyed. I have not attempted to explain everything at the end of each story, and the reader is invited to make up his own conclusions.

There are several ways this book can be read: for entertainment, gaining what humor and laughter is available from the experiences of others; to discover insights, concepts and ideas which will enable the reader to become more effective in discipline techniques; or as a read–aloud sharing time with a child.

The reader would be ill-advised to accept everything I have written and attempt to practice it. What works for one may fail for another. David, after trying on Saul's armor, wisely took it off before facing Goliath (*1 Samuel 17:38, 39*).

The actual writing of a book is an experience in discipline; the same can be said of reading one. Without the support of wonderful Christian friends, this book would have been most improbable.

"Pat" Patchen, Executive Secretary of The National Educators Fellowship, Inc., an organization of Christian professional educators, planted the germ in my mind to write, and watered it rigorously with his prayers, letters, and personal pleas. There's just no way a person can say *No* to Pat once he hugs you.

Nancy Stake, Director of Citizens for Scientific Creation, took time from an impossible schedule of duties to read the manuscript and offer suggestions.

The woman's touch is always essential and hers is among the finest. Thank you, Nancy.

—Louis R. Goodgame

P.S. In some stories, I have resorted to fictitious names to protect the guilty. I make no apology for the innocent.

EARLY CHILDHOOD

1. A Baby's Choice

I was born, unlike most babies, not within the confines of an antiseptic hospital, but in the basement tenement of a Polish community. My deliverer was a noble Jewish midwife, a professional in that ancient art of bringing infants properly into a home.

After holding me high in the air and carefully scrutinizing my thrashing body, she made her pronouncement. "Ah, ha, a male child you are blest with, Mrs. Goodgame! Such strong lungs and wisdom in his eyes."

With such an introduction I was eagerly claimed by my mother, for she had no benefit of drugs to dull the joy of giving birth to her firstborn. Just as happily, I snuggled up to a feast of love and maternal nourishment. The midwife left us to our pleasures and announced my safe arrival to a house filled with relatives, friends, neighbors, and passers-by. That is the splendor of a homemade birth; it is a neighborhood event.

The midwife returned to the bedroom for her final inspection and parting blessing. "Your son reminds me of a Bible baby," she proclaimed. Mother's heart surged with pride at this revelation. "Isaac, yes, he's another Isaacal," the Jewess decreed. "I see in him much joy and laughter." With that, the midwife folded her worn hands, bowed, and slipped away to another house call.

Fortunately, with a wisdom beyond her seventeen years, mother decided to name me after my father and not the Biblical patriarch. An "Isaac" would have found life extremely interesting in a Polish neighborhood.

At the "age of crawlability" I was granted the privilege of predicting my destiny. Poles have more confidence in their babies than in crystal balls, tea leaves, or horoscopes. I was set on a bed sheet in the living room, surrounded by relatives. At the edge of the sheet were three enticing objects: a piece of fresh baked bread, a bright silver dollar, and a Polish prayer book. Which treasure would be the goal of my life? All was silent as I lurched forward by inches to seize my guiding star. Sighs of joy filled the room when my chubby hands clutched the sacred book, which was immediately rescued before I attempted to taste the pages.

Pa, my grandfather, nodded his approval and announced that I would be a lover of books and attend college. Busha, my grandmother, added her blessing on my becoming a priest or teacher. Uncle Joe, my godfather, was grateful my ambition would not end up in the food business but had hoped I might have become the family's first banker.

In a mysterious way that some might call chance, but our family gave God the credit, I had been guided to reveal my destiny. Once this awesome choice was made, the family accepted and promised to support my decision. Years later, as was expected, I became the first college graduate of our family and entered the teaching profession.

If you are tempted to try this infant ritual on your next child, for all babies are basically alike in the beginning, please remember two things. First, allow a generous handicap if you are not Polish, for we've had centuries to polish the technique. Second, and most important, never allow your child to forget the decision. Throughout the growing years you must constantly encourage and support the child in the great expectation. For, and this is the subtle secret, not even babies like to admit they made a mistake, except perhaps when it came to selecting their parents.

Discipline Principles

Discipline is dedication, the mental grasping for a desired goal. It is defined as "training which corrects, molds, strengthens, or perfects" *(Webster's New Collegiate Dictionary)*.

Of all disciplines, the teachings of Christ contain the greatest challenge and the highest attainment. In His Sermon on the Mount, Christ encouraged great expectations: "Be ye therefore perfect, even as your Father which is in heaven is perfect" *(Matthew 5:48;* King James version will be used unless otherwise identified).

Discipline is discipleship, the following of a chosen master. This hope for perfection, the quest for the best, is portrayed by John: "Oh, dear children of mine (forgive the affection of an old man!), have you realized it? Here and now we are God's children. We don't know what we shall become in the future. We only know that, if reality were to break through, we should reflect his likeness, for we should see him as he really is! Everyone who has at heart a hope like that keeps himself pure, for he knows how pure Christ is" *(1 John 3:2,3; Phillips).*

Discipline Practices

Parents have an obligation to expect good and great things of their children. Such desires indicate our love, and even more important, they help the child develop a positive image of self-worth.

The extreme of expecting "too much—too often" of the child is to be avoided, for the impossible dream quickly reverts to the possible nightmare. The opposite error of expecting "too little—too seldom" is also damaging. Children are crippled by the implication that they are underachievers and unable to cope with failure.

The parental instinct to shield children from failure can ensnare them in a cocoon of apathy. A child restricted to the shallow end of the pool, where the water barely reaches the ankles, will never learn to swim.

In dealing with defeat and apparent failure, a few basic rules need to be reviewed:

Failure is relative. Everyone fails, but not to the same depth or degree. Jesus was careful to explain this concept to Pilate when He pointed out that Judas had the "greater sin" (see *John 19:11*). In the growing–learning process, children often mar the wood and bend the nail as they hammer away at adulthood. Why do we insist that he be a man when all that nature requires is that he be a boy?

Failure is deceptive. Failure delights to dwell within the eye of the beholder. To insure failure in others, and excuse it in ourself, we see with selectivity. The home-run records of Babe Ruth and Henry Aaron can be failurized when we focus on their number of strikeouts and times at bat.

Failure is democratic. Failure is one of the few democratic principles left to the world today. It is no respecter of persons, positions, or practices. Wealth, health, and education may appear to impede its progress at times, but this delay is deceptive. The longer one waits for failure, the more failure one has to expect.

Failure is regressive. Failure is true to itself and refuses to recognize success under any conditions or in any form. Given enough failures, however, success is inevitable. The pure essence of failure is distilled when one finally fails to fail.

Failure is reactionary. Children learn from their parents to love, accept, and attempt; they reflect our feelings and values. Too often they resist the risk necessary for success, fearful that failure will jeopardize their stature in the home. To accept your children, especially when they fail, is a stronger expression of love than to praise them when they succeed. The parents' attitude and reaction determine the role that failures will play in their child's development.

Discipline Proverbs

- A child who has nothing to crawl for has plenty to crawl from.

- The fear to begin is in itself the final end.

- You buy a runt when you sell your child short.

- A little defeat prepares for a greater victory.

- Children rarely disappoint parents who expect little or nothing from them.

2. *Chicken Tears*

I was at the awesome age of three, yet the memory is still fresh and crisp, when mother taught me some rudiments of family discipline. We were spending the summer on grandfather's Wisconsin farm.

Of all the barnyard animals, the hogs captivated my imagination. I had been warned never to feed them unless an adult was with me, but their eating habits proved irresistible. I was caught in the very act of dragging the slop-pail toward the pigs' sty and promptly delivered to mother for punishment. The fact that I had not actually dumped the swill on my friends was no defense, as my clutching the bucket indicated open defiance in the first degree.

"Junior," mother explained, "since my words did not impress you, perhaps grandfather's razor strap will."

It certainly did!

Apparently my wails of woe had little visible effect on mother, for she invited me to continue my upheavals elsewhere. I stomped out of the house and sat on the back porch in full abjection. Tears rolled off my quivering cheeks to die in muddy graves of the summer's dust. As the pain in my extremities diminshed, I became aware of someone's presence. Hopefully I looked up, thirsting for sympathy, only to see an ancient hen of the Rhode Island Red tribe gawking at me.

"What you lookin' at?" I whimpered.

She refused to answer, but did slyly blink an orange eye at me. The thought of being left to the ridicule of a stupid chicken maddened my mind. In a fit of fury I poured forth the most agonizing scream my rested lungs could muster. It worked. Mother dashed out of the house in panic, certain that I had been kidnapped by timber wolves.

"Junior!" she cried in relief at finding me still available, "what happened?"

I clutched her tightly, letting my tears speak for themselves. It was such a wholesome feeling to be noticed, loved, and protected; besides, seeing mother upset was just compensation for my recent pain. All this goodness ended when mother demanded an explanation for my outburst.

"The chicken looked at me," I whimpered.

"The what!" she roared.

I sensed displeasure and hastened to explain. "That there chicken," I pointed out the guilty fowl, "looked at me."

"Am I to understand that you screamed because that poor hen happened to look at you?" she demanded.

Old enough to realize that any further facts would only be held against me, I nodded my confession of guilt. While my pants were being lowered, for another introduction to Mr. Razor Strap, mother explained the facts of life.

"Junior, you're not to cry and scream unless there's a good reason to do so."

"Yes, Momma," I heartily agreed, hoping to soften the blows.

"When you're hurt or afraid, then it's all right to

cry, for such tears are pure and true. But when you cry over nothing, these are fake tears, do you understand?"

"Yes, Momma."

"Mother doesn't want her boy to waste his tears, so now I must give you something you can honestly cry over."

Once again I found myself alone on the back porch, making tear puddles in the dust. When the pain had dulled sufficiently, my mind was clear enough to cast all blame on that conniving chicken. I immediately set out in hot pursuit to avenge my wrongs. Vengeance was not to be mine, however, for that stupid bird had retreated to the safety of the flock where all Rhode Islanders look alike.

Discipline Principles

Tears, whether they be of joy or anguish, should truthfully express one's feelings. Children quickly learn the power of tears to gain attention, win one's desires, and to escape punishment. As long as crying, sobbing, and whining have such rewards, they will be practiced to perfection. Even Esau, the outdoor hunter, reverted to tears in an attempt to gain back his birthright:

> For you know that even afterwards, when he desired to inherit the blessing, he was rejected, for he found no place for repentance, though he sought for it with tears (*Hebrews 12:17, NASB*).

Discipline Practices

Learn to distinguish and react to the different types of crying, such as: pain, anger, fear, frustration, desire for attention, and even boredom.

Solomon was careful to explain that there is a proper "time to weep" *(Ecclesiastes 3:4)*. "Jesus wept" *(John 11:35)*, giving a manly example of this form of expression. Children, having a just cause for crying, should receive prompt attention, love, and relief of pain. These comforts should not suddenly cease when the crying stops, but should linger on. Avoid the impression that crying must always precede loving attention, or children will be tempted to enlarge upon their griefs.

Rewarding fake tears with tender attention will only insure their steady supply. Under such dampening conditions there are different corrective techniques available:

- Ignore them. Providing your patience and nerves are up to it, let them cry, but strictly alone. Engulfed in their deceptions, the novelty will soon simmer down to an occasional whimper. Wait them out, and hold back your affections until they have stopped this mischief. It is gratifying to observe how quickly they learn that hypocrisy hath little reward.

- Give them something to really cry for. A firm warning should be given, consisting of two parts: *Part the first:* Since there is nothing to be crying for, you will immediately cease from this activity. *Part the second:* If you choose not to stop crying, I shall respect your decision and make it worthwhile by giving you something to honestly cry over. This parental advice should only be given once, as repetition will only weaken your position and strengthen a child's rebellion. Should they heed your advice, and stop crying, you are free to reward their obedience. If they persist in crying, positive paddling will bring a ring of sincerity to their performance and allow you to express genuine concern for their comfort.

Discipline Proverbs

- "Foolishness is bound in the heart of a child; but the rod of correction shall drive it far from him (King Solomon, *Proverbs 22:15*).

- "... and the joy of the hypocrite but for a moment?" (Zophar the Namathite, *Job 20:5*).

- Nature put a grain of salt in every teardrop, so take each one that way.

3. Woolworth Wail-out

At the age of four, I experienced another example of mother's discipline which left her mark on me.

For being a good boy, mother rewarded me with a trip to the local Woolworth store and the privilege of selecting one ten cent toy. I am of the opinion that more parental authority has been lost in Woolworth dime stores than probably any other public structure. (Not that Woolworth is the chief offender; any modern shopping center will provide equal opportunity for rebellion.)

Mother deposited me at the toy counter under strict orders to remain there awaiting her return. Actually, wild hippos couldn't have enticed me from those treasures. My serious meditations were abruptly violated by a small boy and his mother. This mannerless male shoved me rudely aside and began grabbing toys wholesale. His mother pleaded for moderation, but to no avail. I was shocked by his behavior, yet fascinated by the amount of plunder it produced.

"Rupert," the mother sniffed, "don't you think you've quite enough toys?"

He never gave her the courtesy of a reply as he continued to rip toys off the counter and fling them into her out-stretched shopping bag.

"Rupert, dearest," she pleaded, "unless you come with me this very instant, I shall be forced to speak to your father." Rupert merely glared and kept on grabbing. "Now, Rupert," she cautioned, "perhaps father shall be so upset with your conduct that he might even be forced to spank—"

She never finished. At the very mention of the word "spank," Rupert went into instant insanity. With a screech he hurled himself head-long to the floor, kicking and thrashing like a snake in a lawn mower. *He was magnificent!*

Rupert's mother immediately dropped to his stricken side, sobbing apologies for having hurt his finer sensibilities. All sorts of desserts and bribes were promised if he'd only stop screaming and be a good boy. Rupert's recovery was as remarkable as his affliction. He hopped to his feet and filled the shopping bag, then dragged mother to the candy counter. At the time, I thought their togetherness, each attached to the shopping bag between them, was pure tenderness.

Rupert's theatrics were not wasted, as I was inspired to use the same act on my mother. It seemed most logical that she would be too embarrassed to punish me in public, especially in the presence of strangers. The walk home would also work to my advantage, allowing time to cool her ardor. Besides, unlike Rupert, I would only request one additional toy. I was positive that mother would reward such unselfishness.

I went into action. From the vast array of toys I selected two, a blue Model A car and a red World War I German Fokker airplane. My expectations were so great that I forgot mother's command to stay at the toy counter and I sought her out in the "no man's land" of women's wear.

"Mommie," I gushed, "these are the toys I want."

"Junior," she reminded, "why didn't you wait for me at the toy counter?"

"I'm sorry," I explained, "but I just wanted these toys."

"Well, all right," mother replied, "give me the one you want and take the other back and wait for me there like I told you."

I was apprehensive at mother's blindness to my needs, but with the success of Rupert still music in my ears, I pressed on. "But, Mommie," I begged, "I've been such a good boy, can't I have two toys?"

"Do what I told you," she said firmly.

A small group of spectators began to collect and I gathered courage from their presence. The moment of truth had come, I stood my ground.

"If words fail to move you," mother warned, "I might have to spank ..."

Spank! The magic word, and like Rupert I responded on cue. With a shriek I dropped to the floor, noting with satisfaction the startled expression on mother's face. I had just begun to thrash when I felt her tender hands lifting me to my feet. "It worked!" I thought, as I helpfully turned toward the direction of the cash register. Then, all came crashing down as mother re-wrote the ending. Her actions were shockingly swift and professionally pure as she stripped my short pants to my ankles and upended me over her knee. In this woefully exposed position, I received personal tutoring.

"Lesson one," she spoke as her hand descended, "if words won't move you, something else will."

I immediately took this lesson to heart and elsewhere.

"Lesson two," she continued, "whenever you cry for something, you won't get it."

Both of us were now warming up to the subject at hand.

"Lesson three," she concluded, "toys are not worth crying over, so I shall provide you with something worthy of your tears."

I cried, honestly and unashamedly, with mother's full approval. Lessons reinforced, she set me upright, restoring my pants to their former honor, which now barely covered my embarrassments. I looked to the crowd for some shred of sympathy, but I stood alone. Even Rupert would have disowned me for the way I had botched the job.

"Take one toy back," mother gently reminded me.

I recognized this as a command, not a request, but rebellion dies hard, even in a four-year-old. I gave it one final shot. "Mommie," I pleaded, "can't I have both toys since you've already spanked me for them?"

A ripple of admiration came from the crowd, but my mother was not to be intimidated. "Junior," she explained, "one toy is yours for being good, you earned that toy. But for the other toy you were naughty, and I'm not going to give you a toy for being bad."

A wave of praise burst forth from the multitude. Even Solomon would have been impressed at mother's wisdom. "Now be a good boy and take one toy back," mother urged.

In full view of the admiring throng, I obeyed. We left Woolworth's together. With one hand I held my toy, the other clutched my mother. Somehow I knew as never before how much she loved me.

Even today, when I enter a dime store, memories of my mother's firmness tickle my heart, especially if the Ruperts are still practicing their profession. For who else but a real mother could have taught her son a million-dollar lesson in a dime store?

Discipline Principles

Throughout recorded history the problem of parental authority has been discussed and bemoaned. All nations in all ages have grappled with this universal inclination to disobey and defy parents. A clay tablet unearthed in Mesopotamia had this comment on family affairs around 3,000 B.C.

> The times are intolerable. Children no longer obey their parents. Everybody wants to write a book. Surely the world must be coming to an end!

That future generations would also share this situation was predicted by the Apostle Paul.

> This know also, that in the last days perilous times shall come. For men shall be lovers of their own selves ... proud ... disobedient to parents ... *(2 Timothy 3:1, 2)*.

The Bible contains examples, both positive and negative, of how parents raised their children. While Adam and Eve were successful with Abel and Seth, they had difficulties in raising Cain. Two fathers, Abraham and Eli, reveal some insights as to effective fatherhood.

■ Eli—a failure as a father. Whatever his methods, Eli lost out in rearing both his sons, Hophni and Phinehas. The people called these boys the "sons of Belial" *(1 Samuel 2:12)*, and their religious practices would have caused the heathen to blush (*1 Samuel 2:13–17, 22*). Eli appealed to them by asking, "Why do ye such things?" (*1 Samuel 2:23*). The Scripture records their concerted response: "Notwithstanding they hearkened not unto the voice of their father . . ." (*1 Samuel 2:25*).

- Abraham—a successful father. One of the closest relationships between father and son is that of Abraham and Isaac. Fatherhood didn't come easy or early to Abraham, who was one hundred years old when Isaac arrived (*Genesis 21:5*). The test of their love came on top of a lonely mountain in the land of Moriah. There, a sorrowful father tried to explain to his young son that he was to become a human sacrifice. Isaac did not argue, plead, struggle, or attempt escape. A young man, thirsting for life, he still remained a son and submitted to death itself. Why? Because of duty, his deep sense of obedience, or because of his love?

How was Abraham able to raise an Isaac and Eli only a Phinehas? What made the difference between these ancient patriarchs? The Bible gives an indication of the basic difference between these men:

- Abraham commanded: "For I know him, that he will command his children and his household after him . . ." (*Genesis 18:19*).

- Eli questioned: "Why do ye such things?" (*1 Samuel 2:23*).

Discipline Practices

In an open confrontation over parental authority, a firm stand must be taken and maintained. Any direct attack by the child on the parental role and position cannot go unchecked or be ignored. Sooner or later parents will be forced into action as the child will press and push until they react.

Children often interpret the permissive attitude in parents as a sign of rejection or disinterest. They may defy and rebel in order to know if their parents really care enough to correct.

Be careful to distinguish between open defiance and childish neglect. There is a vast difference between Johnny forgetting to feed the dog and a challenge of "I will not!" when told to do so.

Do not construe every question and disagreement as open mutiny, for to disagree does not always mean to disrespect. Children are naturally curious, for by curiosity they learn and acquire knowledge. They also enjoy a good argument as much as their parents do. Allow them to express their opinions and convictions in a respectful manner. Be mature enough to accept and praise their good ideas; it's a wise parent who learns from children. Adult authority is easier for children to accept when they feel their views have at least been heard and considered.

A sudden outburst of rebellion is often the outer symptom of an inner conflict. Suppose Sally refuses to wash the dishes, a normal chore she has performed in the past without defiance. Her mother can ignore the flare-up and wash the dishes herself, but Sally's basic problem remains. Or she can force Sally to wash the dishes, but this will not clean up Sally's troubles. A sincere attempt should be made to find out why Sally doesn't want to wash the dishes, what is upsetting her over such a simple task. She may not be able to explain or understand her frustrations, but mother's willingness to take time to talk and help will be appreciated.

Temper tantrums can be highly embarrassing, which is precisely why children (and adults) find them so rewarding. Over the centuries, parents have devised several techniques for tempering tantrums:

Bribery and reward. This method is ineffective since the child is rewarded for poor behavior. If you feel compelled to use this aspirin approach, at least refine it to a more corrective experience. Learn to anticipate your child's explosions and reward him *before* he hits the floor. Make it clear that this unexpected goodie is for being a good boy.

For example: Johnny has been derailing the family's life style. To subdue his activities, you have given him a book to look at quietly in the corner. After some ten minutes of page turning, a glance reveals that the book has served its purpose; Johnny is rapidly approaching boredom and upheaval. Don't wait. Praise him for looking at the book so nicely and give him a reward. Three things have been accomplished: the tantrum has been nipped, good behavior rewarded, and some semblance of parental authority exercised.

Ignore and ostracize. Whenever privacy is possible without physical danger, leave the child alone with his emotional endeavors. The family should ignore the culprit, or exile him to another location should his antics prove overbearing. This isolation is exactly what the child doesn't want.

As soon as the child returns to respectability, welcome him back into the family fold. Should his restoration prove premature, and another outburst ensue, be quick to apply banishment. "I'm sorry," you can apologize, "I thought you were finished and ready to return." Send him away, but let the prodigal know that you are awaiting his return.

Prompt punishment. Inform the child that he cannot have what he's hysterical over. If he continues to ferment, command in a calm voice that he cease this nonsense. If the child refuses to comply, reveal that a privilege has been removed. If the child is bound and determined to enjoy this enterprise, if only from all the new found attention it has produced, the ultimate weapon must now be unlimbered and loaded. (For more details on punishment, review the **Appendix:** *Specifications for Spanking.*)

Discipline Proverbs

- "If you refuse to discipline your son, it proves you don't love him; for if you love him you will be prompt to punish him" (*Proverbs 13:24, LB*).

- "Only a fool despises his father's advice; a wise son considers each suggestion" (*Proverbs 15:5, LB*).

- It is easier for a father to become a pal, than for a pal to become a father.

- Whipping should be the last resort and not the first recourse.

- The sooner you learn to reason with a child, the more reasonable he becomes.

4. The Godfather

At my church christening, Uncle Joe became my godfather. He was well qualified to protect me, having been a professional boxer and served in the United States Navy. Uncle Joe took his responsibility seriously, including the matter of my religious training. When of age, I found myself attending Sunday school and church on a regular basis.

During the Great Depression, we lived in Baker, Washington. There was only one local church, a non-denominational group that met in the public schoolhouse. Each Sunday, Catholics, Protestants, and Unclassified worshipped together for the common good.

Going to church in a schoolhouse was both a novelty and a temptation. It was rather difficult to sit silently like a saint in the same desk where I had invented mischief all week at school. Had I been alone, it might have been possible, but the presence of my schoolmates contaminated me, and I them.

Sunday school was actually enjoyable. We met in the basement next to the coal furnace, which was off-limits during regular school. There was an atmosphere of freedom in Sunday school; we could ask questions, play Bible games, and even laugh on occasion. Our teacher was a farmer, Conrad Sture, a veteran of World War I. He had that mystic quality of loving little boys without any apparent effort or even minor irritation.

However, church service was considered on the same level as a trip to the dentist, and we referred to it as the "eleventh hour." Somehow, the sermons seemed long on words and short on interest. We were expected to sit straight, behave like gentlemen, and not make funny faces at each other.

Perhaps the worst feature of holding church in a public school was the location of the clock. This venerable instrument was hung high on the wall directly behind the teacher's desk, thereby insuring that all students would be instilled with the value of time. Our teacher had no difficulty knowing the hour under this arrangement since she had eyes in the back of her head. Unfortunately, the minister was not as wonderfully constructed, and he took full advantage of this disability. Most Sundays, with the clock safely behind him, he blissfully exhorted past the noon hour whilst us young sinners could only view the squandered time in dumb anguish. From this childhood experience I quickly discovered the basic difference between teachers and preachers.

Church decorum required that we look at the minister through a countenance mingled with rapture and discomfiture. Time stood still, but I sat otherwise, twisting for more satisfying scenery to contemplate.

The object of my search never failed to impress me with the blessings of adulthood. Sooner or later I would espy the benign expression of a sleeping saint (sinners never slept during church) and by a system of bodily movements I passed this information on to my schoolmates. Within seconds the little lambs would all be fondly gazing upon our hero, knowing that such concerted attention would not go unrewarded. The poor man's wife, finally sensing our stares, would apply a rude elbow into his ribs. His sudden awakening and attempts to salvage some dignity rejoiced our hearts and stimulated a rash of muffled giggles.

On a Sunday when my conduct had humiliated the family name, I dreaded to return home. Uncle Joe always demanded a full report on our religious experience and his favorite question seemed to be about me. When informed of my misdeeds, punishment was swift and sore. Normally, Uncle Joe didn't whip on Sundays, this being the day of rest, but he always managed to find a suitable substitute.

For the hour I wasted in church two hours of practice were decreed on the camel-back steamer trunk. Thus exiled in the living room, under orders of strict silence, I served my time. Several such sessions soon taught me that a humped trunk is nothing to be trifled with.

During these periods of punishment I had ample opportunity to ponder my conduct in church. I certainly had better things to do on a Sunday afternoon, especially when my buddies would drop by on their way to go swimming at Salmon Creek. The lesson was finally etched in my mind and behind that it was better to sit quietly in church for one hour than to waste two hours on a bumpy trunk. Once this germ of truth infected my brain, the battle was won, and since this was my very own decision, I found it to my liking.

Discipline Principles

Discipline is based upon decisions. As soon as possible and whenever possible, give a child a chance to make decisions. Discipline, by its very nature, is often distasteful; we all tend to rebel when dictated to. Given a choice, even that meager morsel of deciding between the lesser of two evils, and discipline becomes digestible.

Moses guided a multitude of ex-slaves for about forty years in the wilderness. They should have been docile, having been trained to obey, but docility was left in the Red Sea. This remarkable transformation of an entire nation is difficult to explain. Why weren't they happy and content with their new-found freedom? Why did they continually threaten to return to Egypt and slavery as recorded in *Numbers 14:4?* There are several rationalizations of their behavior:

- Too strict + too long = too loose. As slaves they had been bound in body and soul, contained and controlled too tightly. Once the restraints were removed, they exploded under freedom. The proverbial preacher's son who suddenly abandons his strict training for riotous living illustrates this theory.

- Use it or lose it. Under bondage the Israelites had little opportunity to make decisions. This lack of practice dulled their talent to choose wisely.

Israel lacked the practice and growth which comes from making a decision and then learning to live with it. This responsibility was suddenly thrust upon them, and they often stumbled over it. God was patient and slowly trained them; a life of slavery is not nullified overnight. They made their choices and God honored them, for better or for worse.

After the wilderness wanderings were completed, and a new generation had emerged, God continued to set decisions before His children. On Mt. Gerizim were pronounced the blessings and from Mt. Ebal the cursings (see *Deuteronomy 27–30).* Moses concluded with this challenge: "I call heaven and earth to record this day against you, that I have set before you life and death, blessing and cursing: therefore *choose* life, that both thou and thy seed may live . . ." *(Deuteronomy 30:19).*

Once the Promised Land had been obtained, Joshua again offered a choice to the people: "And if it seem evil unto you to serve the Lord, *choose* you this day whom ye will serve; whether the gods which your fathers served that were on the other side of the flood, or the gods of the Amorites in whose land ye dwell: but as for me and my house, we will serve the Lord" *(Joshua 24:15).*

God does not force or intimidate. He sets before us both sides of the issue and allows us the privilege to think and decide for ourselves.

The urge to make our children good can blind us to the foolishness of force. We may coerce children to obey, but this is a temporary condition which they quickly outgrow. There are three basic philosophies to choose from in the realm of raising children:

- Dictatorial. "Strain up a child in the way he should go: and just as soon as he's old enough he will depart from it and from you" *(Cave Man Chronicles,* Chapter 1).

- Permissive. "Refrain not a child in any way he desires to go: and when he is old enough to be a man he'll still be a child" *(The Now Society,* Chapter 3).

- Rational. "Train up a child in the way he should

go: and when he is old, he will not depart from it"
(The Proverbs, Chapter 22, Verse 6, by Solomon).

Train, strain, or never refrain: the choice is
ours, the result theirs.

Make the punishment fit and correct the crime.
In the Ten Commandments, God gave a simple but
complete code by which society could survive and
prosper. One of these commandments is the simple
statement, "Thou shalt not steal" *(Exodus 20:15).*
Later, God gave Israel a set of civil laws, included
in which were the punishments for stealing:

- Punishment for non-returnable stolen property:
  "If a man steals an ox or a sheep, and slaughters it
  or sells it, he shall pay five oxen for the ox and
  four sheep for the sheep" *(Exodus 22:1, NASB).*

- Punishment for returnable stolen property: "If
  what he stole is actually found alive in his posses-
  sion, whether an ox or a donkey or a sheep, he
  shall pay double" *(Exodus 22:4, NASB).*

God's punishment for stealing not only fit the
crime, an ox for an ox, but it strongly motivated correction by restoring more than had been stolen.
What would happen to organized crime if offenders
had to return from double up to five times the
amount stolen? Rehabilitation of robbers will not be
achieved by confinement in jails, but it can be
realized by this basic principle of restoration plus.
Once the profit is taken out of crime the criminals
will be intelligent enough to find a better way.

Develop proper motives for punishment. Motives for punishing children come in all shapes and
sizes. It is difficult to punish effectively if we begin
with a poor motive.

- Revenge. This is self-satisfaction at its very worst, the desire to get even with our children whose untimely arrival ruined our life-style.

- Authority. As parents we must maintain our position and never let the children forget who is boss.

- Justice. The law demands that crimes and criminals must be punished.

- Protection. Suitable punishment will deter future infractions, thereby protecting the innocent.

- Correction. The wrongdoer must be reformed and rehabilitated for his own good.

- Restoration. The desire that after all is said and done, both guilty and innocent will be drawn closer together in understanding and love.

Discipline Practices

Effective punishment begins with the right motive which is followed up with correct methods. Here are some common problems most parents face in training their children:

Donald and the door. Donald is so excited to get outside to play that he constantly leaves the door open when leaving the house, or when reminded, slams it shut. There are several steps to the solution.

- Explanation. There are good reasons for closing the door when leaving the house which children can appreciate. The need to conserve energy, avoid the invasion of insects, and keep neighborhood pets out of the food should suffice for the discerning child.

- Demonstration. Show the proper way that ladies and gentlemen close a door when leaving a house. Children appreciate parents who take the time to explain and teach by example. It's also nice to inform them that as a child you had the same problems and your parents had to instruct you in the arts of adulthood.

- Practice under supervision. Assign a specific number of times for the child to open and completely close the door. This initial practice should be reasonable in number of times required, not more than ten. Should the child decide to test the system and do a sloppy job, don't interrupt his foolishness and get into a vocal argument over the rights or wrongs of his method.

- Evaluation. After the practice is completed a vocal evaluation is necessary. Be liberal with praise for a job well done and allow him to continue on his course to the great outdoors. However, if he has not taken this lesson seriously, express your disappointment and indicate that apparently more practice is required. *Avoid argument,* simply demonstrate again the proper way of closing a door and assign another practice session longer in length. Usually, a second effort has a most wholesome effect, but should the child persist in defiance, you can react by: assigning additional practice sessions until it is apparent this method is ineffective, then quickly change tactics; informing the child that it appears he is not ready at the moment to go outdoors. Confine the child to the house for a specific period of time, say thirty minutes, after which you'll be most willing to see if an improvement has taken place.

■ Follow-up reinforcements. Make it a point to observe your child leaving the house and closing the door correctly so that you can heap coals of praise upon his head. Habits, good or bad, once formed are most difficult to break.

Cathy and her clothes. Cathy hardly ever hangs up her clothes and merrily strews them throughout the house. The odds are in her favor as someone will usually pick them up and at the very worst she'll only have to hang them herself. Like Donald, Cathy needs some practice in hanging and unhanging her clothes, be they levis or formal attire.

Discipline Proverbs

■ If you refuse to think for yourself, someone will gladly do it for you.

■ Praise insures repetition of the same action.

5. Belteshazzar*

"UP!"

With that single syllable, Pa, my grandfather, awoke me each morning precisely at 6:00 a.m., including the day I made the fatal error. While fumbling my eight-year-old body into work clothes, Pa departed for the barn to prepare Sookie, the family cow. He gave her special food to eat, washed her udder, and checked nipples for cracks. The actual milking was my responsibility.

There is something therapeutic about sitting on a stool, close to the warmth of a contented bovine. The rhythmic surging of milk entering the pail is tranquilizing; the sense of power in squeezing forth the frothy foam is gratifying. After milking, I carried the bucket to cousin Bob at the separator. This mechanical marvel, merely by turning the crank, poured pure cream from one spout and skim milk from the other.

My next task was to open the chicken house to let out the fowls for their breakfast of grain. The final job was to fill Busha's woodbox on the back

---

*Belteshazzar: The Babylonian name of a famous Hebrew who appreciated keeping company with those who had "closed mouths."

porch. (Busha is the Polish way to say grandmother.)
This required several trips as she was a dedicated
wood-burner and demanded a hot fire for cooking,
baking, and washing. Her bread was the delight of
the community.

When my morning chores were completed, I
then washed, changed into school clothes, and ate
breakfast. Since every man, woman, and child had
already worked, appetites needed no encouragement. With a full stomach and somewhat tired body
I left for school, grateful for the chance to rest and
play. Thus began the day at the Sadowski farm.

However, at the enlightened age of eight I decided to rebel against this slavery of chores before
breakfast. One morning after Pa awakened me, I
crawled back under the feather quilt satisfied that a
growing body requires more sleep and less toil.

I was totally asleep when Pa returned. I was
semi-asleep when he dragged me from my derelic-
tions and positioned me on the floor. I was totally
awake the instant his leather belt collided with my
personal property.

"Awake?" Pa inquired.

"Yes! Yes! Yes!" I howled.

Pa calmly watched me tear into my work
clothes as he replaced that dreaded symbol of authority. Dressed, I dashed to the barn and unthink-
ingly thrust my bruised flesh upon the stool. Such
sudden contact revived the anguish and forced me
to milk from a squatting position.

The rest of the morning was a blur as I tried to
make up the lost time. Timidly, I approached the
breakfast table ten minutes late to receive my second rude awakening of the morning. The family was
firmly entrenched behind full plates, leaving only
bits and crumbs for my sustenance. I now realized

the folly of not being at the table in time to fend for myself.

Discipline Principles

Develop a work ethic. At an early age children should be taught to work and handle simple responsibilities. There is no substitute for the dignity bequeathed to those who labor to earn their daily bread. Paul expresses this basic principle in these words: "... this we commanded you, that if any would not work, neither should he eat" *(2 Thessalonians 3:10).*

In the Hebrew economy, God made ample provision for the needs of the poor people who were without work. The welfare laws, proclaimed by Moses, removed all excuses for starvation. Here are a few samples of God's plan for protecting the poor.

- Anyone had access to free food for himself. "When you enter your neighbor's vineyard, then you may eat grapes until you are fully satisfied, but you shall not put any in your basket" *(Deuteronomy 23:24, NASB).*

- The disciples of Jesus practiced this law as recorded in *Matthew 12:1.*

- The poor had a portion of the main harvest. "Now when you reap the harvest of your land, you shall not reap to the very corners of your field ... you shall leave them for the needy and for the stranger. I am the Lord your God" *(Leviticus 19:9, 10, NASB).* It was under this law that Ruth, the Moabitess, gleaned in the fields of Boaz *(Ruth 2:2–8).*

- Only the poor could glean after the harvest *(Deuteronomy 24:20,21).*

- Only the poor could harvest fields on the seventh year *(Exodus 23:10,11)*.

In my seventh grade history class we study a unit on Hebrew history based on the Old Testament. Part of this unit is a comparison of "welfare laws" of the Hebrews, Romans and modern America. The students discover the various methods governments have used to reduce the problem of poverty.

- Ancient Rome. As Rome conquered and expanded her empire the increase of cheap labor by slaves and cheap food from the provinces put the small Roman farmers out of work. These unemployed flocked to the cities where the government provided cheap housing, free food (called the "dole"), and gladiator fights for entertainment. As the welfare rolls increased, taxes rose to support this system, which finally fell under its own weight of greed, corruption, boredom, and revolution.

- Modern America. There are many causes for unemployment, such as physical conditions, racial discrimination, lack of education, and automation. The government provides funds for the poor and needy through local welfare and federal Social Security programs. There are also job programs and education.

- The Ancient Hebrews. The civil codes given from God to Moses were simple and specific in their protection of the poor and needy. Throughout these laws was a basic philosophy of work. While food was available and free to the Hebrew poor, they had to go out into the fields and gather it.

My students have been quick to discover this fundamental difference in the welfare programs.

Avoid needless vocalizations. Parents who continually repeat commands are conditioning their children to ignore and neglect. The child, from long experience, knows that nothing will really happen until the parent's voice attains a distinctive volume and pitch (commonly called screaming), before any real action takes place. In effect, the child is saying with your blessing, "Nothing you say is important until you utter it with a generous loss of self-control." Soon, every command, be it ever so simple and reasonable, results in a crisis.

Parents must develop the ability to speak softly, firmly, and finally. Jesus clearly rejected the use of "vain repetitions" as an instrument of persuasion *(Matthew 6:7)*.

Encourage children to be responsible by depending on them. Responsibility takes on a new meaning when we sincerely feel needed and necessary. To be depended upon is one of the sweeter satisfactions of life. Since children are limited in what they can do for their parents, we should be careful not to cut off these avenues of dependency.

Parents need children. Children need parents. And both need to know that they are needed. The deepest request any parents can make is to say, "My son, give me thine heart" *(Proverbs 23:26)*.

Discipline Practices

While chores are easier to come by in the country, a little ingenuity can provide city families with daily responsibilities. Here are a few work assignment ideas:

- Baby-sitting and child care
- Car cleaning and repairs
- Clothes: making and mending
- Energy conservation: checking on lights, heat
- Garbage and trash disposal
- House cleaning: daily, weekly, yearly
- Meal and table preparation and cleanup
- Repairs: appliances, furniture, toys
- Pets: feeding, grooming, training
- Shopping for food, clothes, especially checking for sales
- Washing: clothes, dishes
- Yard work: leaves, grass, weeds

Children who fail to work and handle responsibilities at home face a disadvantage when they seek employment. Do a little less around the home so that your children can do a little more for you and themselves.

Discipline Proverbs

- No one is so wealthy that he can afford to become workless.
- What the ears ignore can strike you in the end.
- Whatever fails isn't worth repeating.
- Few things are more foolish than an adult arguing with a child.
- Parents who need children are the happiest parents in the world.

■ "Chastise your son while there is hope for him, but be careful not to flog him to death" *(Proverbs 19:18, NEB).*

6. Pa's Final Word

Every nation has its own peculiar way of expressing anger. These vocal traditions often become rather bland when translated into another language, such as the Englishman's "bloody" or the German's "kauput."

Pa rarely went into a wild wave of passion as he seldom needed to expose his emotions in this manner. A simple "Get out" or "Stop it" was sufficient for most situations. I still remember the one time Pa made my ears tingle.

Pa had gone to a neighbor's farm. With Pa away, Uncle Joe assumed command of the family, and he took his authority seriously. The youngest son, Uncle George, was the family tease and inclined toward books. As is so often the case, his growing intellect increased desires for independence and leadership.

My father, Daddy Pete, and Uncle Joe were grinding valves on the Model A when Uncle George strolled by and offered his services. At first he proved useful, doing simple tasks like scrubbing greasy parts. George soon tired of such menial tasks and demanded better things; even worse, he began to question the competence of his elders and to offer unsolicited advice. Daddy Pete was slightly amused by these adolescent comments but Uncle Joe quickly became incensed at this interference.

"Get in the house with the women," Uncle Joe ordered.

"I won't!" George snapped back sharply, obviously upset at this insult to his manhood.

It was the wrong thing to say; Uncle Joe knew it, I knew it, even George knew it. One simply didn't defy family authority with impunity. Uncle Joe was so startled by George's defiance that he dropped his monkey wrench.

"What did you say?" demanded Uncle Joe.

I was shocked! George was actually being offered a second chance to correct his perfidy, an unusual act of mercy from Uncle Joe. All George had to do was to mumble some incoherent words and retreat to the safety of the house. George, apparently encouraged by the manly grease on his hands, elected to hold his ground.

"You can't make me go!" he shouted.

Fight! There was going to be a fight! In a twinkle the grandchildren, sisters, and brothers stampeded to the front porch which afforded the advantages of safety and a clear view of the gladiators. Since both uncles had punished me in the past, I had no preference as to the victor of this spectacle. Sufficient was my desire that both would be properly pummeled.

"Either you walk to the house," Uncle Joe thundered, "or I'll drag you there."

"Touch me," George screeched, "and I'll straighten your nose!"

It was the ultimate insult. Uncle Joe's nose had been broken during his boxing career, and he was sensitive about its "gawkward" angle. While defiance could be excused on some type of temporary insanity, public ridicule was unforgivable. On both counts George was weighed in the balances and found to be utterly wanting. Uncle Joe began to roll up his sleeves, revealing tattooed muscles. George, not to be outmaneuvered, wisely removed his glasses, and they squared off.

From the smile on Uncle Joe's face I knew that George was in for a generous serving of "Polish Pastry." I sincerely hoped that George would last long enough to land a few blows before being dismantled. Alas, my anticipations were crushed by the sudden arrival of Pa and the neighbor. Pa had witnessed the entire episode as they came down the hill.

"Move back!" Pa ordered his sons.

Pa's unexpected appearance and command startled both brothers into instant inertia. Neither wanted to be the first to break away, so they froze face to face like Greek statues. Immobility proved to be their ruin. Pa had now been openly disobeyed before the family and his neighbor. He swelled with pure fury at this affront to his dignity. It was at this expansion of passion that Pa uttered the most devastating Polish possible: "Dog's blood!"

The actual Polish sound has a distinctive ethnic "k" sound that enhances its harshness. Even a Chinese would have no problem understanding the significance of these syllables. Uncle Joe and George blanched, the children trembled, Busha fled to the bedroom followed by her daughters, and the dog began to chase his tail.

Slowly and deliberately, Pa unbuckled his belt and drew forth that weapon of retribution. I could hardly believe what my eyes insisted was about to transpire. Uncle Joe and George, grown men, were about to be whipped in public! I wondered if they would meekly take their punishment like men or flee like boys? They were both larger and stronger than Pa, and might even strike back. My mind was a turmoil of delight as I watched from the porch hugging my bare legs in excitement.

The look of humiliation and bewilderment by his wayward sons must have placated Pa's wrath. He gave them a second chance to obey.

"I said move!" he repeated, and thrust the belt between their ashen faces for emphasis.

They moved, simultaneously and in opposite directions. George raced to the house while Uncle Joe looked under the Model A for the missing monkey wrench. I felt cheated at their cowardly chicanery. The very least they could have done was to suffer one lash before slinking away in shame. Of one thing I was certain, I had observed a rare lesson of respect for one's father. Whatever schemes I had for testing Pa's authority were drowned in my deepening respect for his personage.

Pa, having restored sanity to the situation, replaced the belt and turned to his neighbor. Poor man, his eyes were still white and wide from what he had witnessed.

"Mr. Sadowski," he gasped, "I never saw anything like that in my life."

"Oh?" Pa questioned, shrugging his broad shoulders.

"You really wouldn't have whipped them, would you?" he asked.

"Sure, I vhip," Pa replied.

"But, Mr. Sadowski," he persisted, "they're grown men!"

Pa shook his head and for the first time the glint of a grin creased his Slavic features.

"Not ven they act like that," was Pa's final word on the matter.

Discipline Principles

Respect for yourself and for others is the foundation of discipline. Solomon describes this relationship in these words: "The fear of the Lord is the beginning of knowledge, but fools scorn wisdom and discipline" *(Proverbs 1:7, NEB)*. The Hebrew word for fear is *Yirah*, which also contains the idea of reverence and respect.

Discipline Practices

True respect begins with a genuine inner feeling that you translate into an outward expression. The basic principles of respect are:

Begin with self-respect. It is very difficult to esteem others if you have a poor estimate of yourself. A good self-image is essential to projecting respect for others. When asked by a lawyer as to which was the greatest commandment, Jesus replied: "Thou shalt love the Lord thy God with all thy heart, and with all thy soul, and with all thy mind. This is the first and great commandment. And the second is like unto it, Thou shalt love thy neighbour as thyself" *(Matthew 22:37–39)*.

Respect is reciprocal. The quantity and quality of the respect you receive is proportional to the respect you bestow. ". . . for them that honour me I will honour, and they that despise me shall be lightly esteemed" *(1 Samuel 2:30)*.

Respect is universal. Everyone, from the innocent child to the hardened criminal, wants respect.

We may not always expect to be understood, appreciated, or loved, but we always expect respect. It is a universal birthright of mankind, our common bond of unity.

As slaves in Egypt the Israelites endured many hardships, including the lack of respect by their masters. God understood this inner need and responded to it: "And God heard their groaning, and God remembered his covenant with Abraham, with Isaac, and with Jacob. And God looked upon the children of Israel, and God had respect unto them" *(Exodus 2:24,25).*

Peter mentions this same concept of total respect for everyone: "Show respect for everyone. Love Christians everywhere. Fear God and honor the government" *(1 Peter 2:17, LB).*

Respect is feasible. Regardless of the individual, environment, or circumstances, you can always find grounds for respect. When Christ was hung on the cross, He had little respect from the multitude; even the two thieves reviled him *(Mark 15:32).* But as the day wore on, one of the thieves saw Jesus in a new light and his respect for Jesus was expressed in these words:

> One of the criminals hanging beside him scoffed, "So you're the Messiah, are you? Prove it by saving yourself—and us, too, while you're at it!" But the other criminal protested. "Don't you even fear God when you are dying? We deserve to die for our evil deeds, but this man hasn't done one thing wrong." Then he said, "Jesus, remember me when you come into your kingdom" *(Luke 23:39–42, LB).*

Respect is complimentary. Good old-fashioned

respect is a piece of praise and a taste of courtesy. A delightful description of respect in action was given by Moses. "You shall rise up before the greyheaded, and honor the aged . . ." *(Leviticus 19:32, NASB).*

Discipline Proverbs

■ To respect means to look up, never down.

■ Look carefully enough at a person and you'll find something to hang your respect on.

■ You never really see yourself in a mirror, only in others.

■ Kick a child's toy and he'll kick your tools.

■ "Honor thy father and thy mother: that thy days may be long upon the land which the Lord thy God giveth thee" *(Exodus 20:12,* the fifth of the *Ten Commandments).*

ELEMENTARY SCHOOL
7. *To Fight or Not to Fight*

"Jack," mother instructed, "be sure to study hard, obey your teacher, and don't get into any trouble."

Mother was laying down the law for my first day at school. I was in an agony to be off and running but stood respectfully for her last minute grooming and commands.

"Take good care of Gloria and be sure to protect her," were mother's final words as I bolted out the door and down the road to Baker School. Our family was new in the area, of Polish extraction, and very poor, which must have caused mother some concern as to our welcome at a new school.

Cousin Gloria and I were both assigned to the first grade, even though I was a year older. This delay in my education was made possible by the city fathers of Miami, Florida. A city ordinance required that all transients had to pay tuition for their children to attend public school. Poverty precluded any formal education for Gloria and myself during our stay in Florida.

At the morning recess a freckle-faced boy began giving Gloria his attentions by chasing her around the playground. I recognized her shrieks and dashed to her rescue.

"Don't chase my cousin," I warned the culprit.

"What's it to ya?" Freckles laughed.

"Just leave her alone," I warned.

The bell rang, ending further argument. At the lunch recess, Freckles was after Gloria again; perhaps her being a new girl fascinated him. He was in hot pursuit when I stepped in to block his ardor. His nose collided and collapsed against my fist, causing blood, tears, and screams to flow in all directions.

Freckles fled to the teacher, Mrs. Lambert, to inform her of my felony while I ordered Gloria to stay away from the boys. Knowing that the teacher would soon seek my whereabouts, I headed for the classroom to accept whatever punishment defenders of damsels are entitled to receive. Mrs. Lambert was just finishing with Freckles' inflamed nose when I entered the room.

"He's the one that busted me," Freckles accused.

"Why did you strike him?" she asked.

"Because he was chasing Gloria."

"Did he hurt Gloria?" she inquired.

"No," I admitted, "but that's because I got him before he caught her."

Mrs. Lambert decided I needed a visit with the principal and conveyed me to Mrs. Gilmore in the next room. Though she was small, Mrs. Gilmore taught the upper grades and had them firmly under control. She listened as Mrs. Lambert explained the circumstances, and then took me aside for correction.

"Young man," she spoke in precise English, "fighting is not permitted at Baker School. However, since you are a new student, I shall overlook your misdeed this time, providing you promise never to fight again."

"If he chases Gloria, I'll have to hit him," I replied as respectfully as I could.

"You will do nothing of the sort!" Mrs. Gilmore commanded.

"Yes, I will, ma'am."

"Are you defying me?" she asked.

"But I have to do what my mother tells me," I explained.

"Am I to understand that your mother ordered you to fight at this school?"

"Oh, no," I explained, "she just told me to protect Gloria."

Mrs. Gilmore seemed to soften as she thought on the matter, and then said softly, "That was a nice thing for your mother to say."

I was grateful that Mrs. Gilmore liked my mother.

"Perhaps I could help you protect Gloria," Mrs. Gilmore suggested. "That's a rather large responsibility."

"You could?" I asked.

"Why of course," she beamed. "If any boy bothers Gloria, you tell me and I'll put a stop to it. I'm sure you'd rather play with the boys than have to watch your cousin."

"Oh, yes!" I confessed.

"That will be all, Jack," she concluded. "Just keep me informed of any problems."

"Thank you," I answered, and then dashed out to salvage what was left of the lunch recess.

On the playground I was immediately set on by classmates who inquired of the number of swats I had received. Freckles was upset at my report and sought out Mrs. Lambert for comfort. By a lucky stroke of fate I had become somewhat of a hero for having blasted Freckles and escaped unscathed. He was considered the teacher's pet since his family was the richest in the community and his father was chairman of the school board.

It was my first day at school, my first fight, and my first trip to the principal. I was fortunate to have a teacher who understood the importance of supporting and praising my mother.

Discipline Principles

Though not always possible, it is best if parents and teachers are united in the discipline of children. In these modern days, children need all the possible help they can receive; the same is true of parents and teachers. "Without consultation, plans are frustrated, but with many counselors they succeed" *(Proverbs 15:22, NASB).*

Discipline Practices

Children are quick to learn the art of "dividing and conquering" parents and teachers to achieve their desires. Here are some ways to avoid this splitting of the ranks.

- Listen carefully to what your child says about school but hold any final judgment or action until you have checked it out with the teacher and principal.

- A good compromise for parents and teachers to agree upon is that teachers shouldn't believe everything children tell about their home life and parents shouldn't believe everything they tell about school life.

- Back up the teacher or parent whenever possible so as to present a united front. Whatever differences exist should be discussed between parents and teachers in private, and not in front of the children.

- If parents tear down the child's respect for his teacher, it will be very difficult for the child to learn under that instructor. In such situations the real loser is the child.

- Parents should realize that discipline at school is not the same as discipline at home. The large number of children involved, the greater number of decisions required, and the need to create an atmosphere conducive for learning demand special rules and techniques.

- Parents should visit the school and learn first hand exactly what the problems and possibilities are. The more parents are involved in school, the better our schools and students will become.

Discipline Proverbs

- United we stand, divided we get stood on.
- Gossip grows on ignorance.
- God created a helping hand, greed shriveled it into a fist.

8. *The Knotted Tongue*

Few experiences are more humiliating to a child than that strange affliction known as stuttering. Like many youngsters, I had an early bout with the knotted tongue.

How I became infected with this malady is unclear. There were no stutterers at school for me to emulate. Perhaps the sudden departure of my parents to Texas, seeking work, triggered an emotional backlash when I was left behind with my grandparents. Whatever the cause, I soon acquired a first class case of wild and weird phonetics, which I shall describe as the "agonies" and the "ecstasies."

The agonies were entirely premeditated and constituted stuttering in the first degree. There was a temporary paralysis to utter a specific word, yet my vocal cords still functioned with other words. How the unspeakable word was selected is a mystery. Sometimes it was long and difficult to pronounce but on other occasions a short easy word was drafted. Whatever the primeval purpose, once my subconscious chose the next victim, I was immediately informed of this decision. I knew the word and I knew I could not speak it.

Now began the real agonies—the race against time to select a suitable substitute before I came to the roadblock. My mind would plunge into a frenzy of verbal gymnastics to discover a replacement which hopefully would be a synonym. Time was the enemy, for I only had a few seconds warning to accomplish this task. Quite often I arrived empty-handed and in desperation would press any word into service, including antonyms. Failure to find a word left only two options: I could skip over to the next word in the sentence, leaving a gap; or I could stand there like a dumb dog with my tongue hanging out. In either event the result was always the same—everybody laughed at me.

The agonies reached their zenith at school during my reading class. Mrs. Lambert's insistence that each word be read exactly as printed destroyed my substituting subterfuge. Under these conditions I was forced to stop abruptly as if my tongue had been impaled. My sudden silence would cause a flurry of hands as students vied for the honor of speaking the word I was incapable of uttering. My only hope with the agonies during reading class was that the unmentionable word would be of sufficient difficulty so as to make my failure respectable. How I hated to be nailed shut on common words like: "that," "almost," and "even."

The ecstasies were crimes of ignorance for which I had no warning or premonition. They fell into two basic patterns, barking and howling.

In barking I would begin a word and then unexpectedly go into a series of fast repetitions. Like a jammed machine gun I would spew forth the same syllables in all directions. Usually, the series of repeats would be reasonable, say three or four, but on some occasions the needle got stuck. Breaking the pattern was accomplished by many and devious methods, such as shouting louder, slapping my hands, stomping my feet, pinching myself, or even combinations of these contortions.

Howling was precisely that—a prolonged wail of the same syllable. My throat would freeze, locking the vocal cords into one vibration pattern capable of producing one and only one sound. Like barking, howling could only be aborted by unique physical movements which only added to the hilarity of the spectators.

My stuttering had a predictable effect among the students—laughter. Such gaiety affected discipline and learning. Finally, Mrs. Lambert asked me to remain after school for speech therapy.

"Jack," she asked, "are you doing anything to stop stuttering?"

"No, ma'am."

"Have your parents mentioned taking you to a doctor?"

"Doctor?" I protested, "I'm not sick."

"Do you stutter at home?" she questioned.

"Yes, and also at church and the neighbors," I answered.

She seemed relieved that school had not been singled out for the expression of my talents. Mrs. Lambert was silent as she considered the next therapy step.

"Jack," she confided, "I really don't mind if you stutter in class, but the children laugh so much that it's making it difficult for me to teach them." I nodded in agreement, grieved that my disability was making life uncomfortable for her.

"Can you think of any times when you don't stutter?" she asked.

I thought, but only one instance came to mind and I blurted it out. "I don't stutter in my dreams!"

"Oh, my," she laughed, "I meant when you're awake."

Her laughter eased the tension and made me feel better. I dug deeper to find another stutterless situation.

"Well, I don't stutter when I talk to the dog."

"Good," she praised, "so you can talk clearly to animals."

"Yes, ma'am."

"Now let's see," she prodded. "Do you stutter when you talk to yourself?"

"You mean out loud?" I asked.

"That's right, when you're all alone."

"Well, usually I just think silent to myself," I answered, "but when I do talk out loud all alone I don't remember stuttering."

"Wonderful!" she gushed, "now we both know that there are times you talk without stuttering."

"But not when I'm around lots of people," I argued.

"We'll work on that, but first you need to practice talking without stuttering. Jack, I want you to talk to yourself, aloud, every day."

My expression fell considerably as I pictured myself being called the village idiot. Even children knew what kind of people went around talking to themselves.

"Jack," Mrs. Lambert pleaded, "don't you want to stop stuttering?"

"Yes," I answered, "but I don't like talking to myself."

"All right then," she offered, "how about reading a book aloud instead. Would you do that?"

"Could I read it alone?"

"Certainly, go out in the barn or in the woods but be sure to read in a loud voice."

I really didn't see how this would help but I was willing to try. Mrs. Lambert allowed me the privilege of selecting several books from her private store and my therapy began.

With a good book tucked under my arm I stole into the forest for this secret medication. The trees became an audience and then after long familiarity, close friends, as they listened in majestic approval. At times, animals seemed to investigate these strange proceedings, but never was I inflicted with laughter or rejection. Sometimes I sat under a favorite friend, comforted by the barky touch upon my shoulders. On special occasions when the book was exciting, I would stand upon a stump and orate Cicero-like to the entire forest.

It worked! By some mystic means, reading aloud in the privacy of Mother Nature had a wholesome effect. My stuttering attacks began to diminish both in size and frequency. Mrs. Lambert was quick to notice my new image and was lavish with her praise, encouragement, and supplies of literature.

Did reading aloud really cure my stuttering or was it coincidental with the real cause for recovery? Regardless of the scientific truth this experience did have some beneficial fringe benefits. I developed a new appreciation for nature and natural surroundings, and I acquired a respect and love for books. My reading ability improved so rapidly that I was promoted to the next grade. Where Florida failed, Washington prevailed. The taste of success was so sweet that I developed an addiction for it. Finally, I was absolutely amazed at the wisdom of teachers and determined to become one.

Discipline Principles

Talk it over. Regardless of the problem or situation, it is essential to take the time to talk it over.

"Come now, and let us reason together ..." *Isaiah 1:18*, contains the two basic ingredients of counseling: reason and together.

Encouragement. The sincere confidence we express in others, by depending upon them, is solid ground on which they can stand and build. This "we can do it together" philosophy was expressed by Caleb when he returned from spying out the Promised Land. "And Caleb stilled the people before Moses, and said, Let us go up at once and possess it; for we are well able to overcome it" *(Numbers 13:30)*.

Personal participation. Spectators may enjoy the game but they never win or lose it. There are times when the services of a professional are required, but no one can substitute for your personal participation. Children want to help, to have a part, to contribute; and their basic needs must find proper channels of expression. When Jesus needed money He involved Peter, using his skill as a fisherman *(Matthew 17:24–27)*. Jesus could have made money out of mud, but instead He asked Peter to participate.

Discipline Practices

Talking things over is important if children are to relate to parental discipline in a positive manner. In talking and counseling with your children:

- Avoid lectures and the attempt to persuade by preaching.

- The use of stories and illustrations will impress your child's mind and remain fresh with him. Stories should be carefully selected and can be read to smaller children, often as a reward for good conduct. Children also enjoy hearing about the adventures of their parents and grandparents. The tales should include defeats as well as victories. Jesus, the Master Teacher, depended on stories (parables) to make His teachings helpful to the people. "But without a parable spake he not unto them ..." *(Mark 4:34)*.

- Be positive and let the child know that regardless of his faults and failings you have not rejected or given up on him.

- Be hopeful and find some evidence of success be it ever so slight or fragile.

- Put yourself in the position of having to depend on the child by having him participate. Feeling needed will stimulate the child to greater efforts.

- Be sincerely generous with your praise not only for your child's success but also for his attempts and his courage during defeat.

Discipline Proverbs

- Talk is often cheap but silence is often expensive.

- You can take a little time to talk now or spend a lot of time crying later.

- One slap on the back is worth more than ten on the behind.

- A child's problem demands a child's solution.

- "When I was a child, I used to talk like a child, and think like a child, and argue like a child ..." *(1 Corinthians 13:11, The Jerusalem Bible)*.

9. A Real McCoy

About a mile from Pa's farm lived a clan of McCoys, straight from the hills of Kentucky. Dad McCoy was a logger and came home only on weekends. He was tall and wiry, and sported a beard that tickled his chest. His words were few, but when he spoke people listened.

The McCoys had a flock of children who ran the farm with their mother while father was away. Bob, the youngest, became my best friend and constant companion.

Saturday night was a big social event with Dad McCoy and he made a family issue of it. I considered it a great honor to be invited to these festivities. We made fudge or popcorn, drank apple cider, and played parlor games. The main entertainment was to coax Dad McCoy to tell us about the famous feud with the Hatfields. He held us enthralled with his picturesque portrayals of hillbilly life and their mountaineer code.

One night, in innocence, I asked how the feud got started. He then related the legendary "pig-tale" episode, which seemed rather humorous now that time has dimmed the tragedy.

"Mr. McCoy," I ventured, "why did you and those Hatfields get so worked up over a few pigs?"

The expression on his face and the way in which he stroked his beard indicated that I was treading on forbidden ground.

"Jack," he replied, "now no pigs is worth killin' over, but a man has to draw the line on what's his and hold onto it."

I nodded my head in full agreement.

"Now we McCoys," he continued, "didn't fuss when they picked a few apples offin our trees, nor complain when they snuck a hen or two. But once they latched onto our hogs, we just knew there'd be no a'stoppin' them."

"That's right!" chorused his sons as Dad McCoy leaned back in his rocking chair.

"You see, Jack, them Hatfields were slavers," Dad McCoy explained. "They fought for the South in the Civil War, but we whipped them good and proper. Since they couldn't have slaves no more, they went after our hogs. Next thing you knowed they'd have itched fer our horses, maybe even our women and children. Why, give those Hatfields enough rope and they might even have spunked up the grit to steal our hounds!"

He was rocking furiously and the creaking added emphasis to his words. "Just no way about it, we had to draw a line at the pigs afore they went after all we had. Understand?"

"Yes, sir," I answered respectfully.

"Sons," Dad McCoy ordered, "get the guns cause I heard them Hatfields in Richfield been jawing after us again!"

"Hatfields in Richfield!" I echoed.

It was my first awareness that the enemy clan was so near at hand. The sons trooped out leaving Dad McCoy, the women folk, and me with a frantically beating heart. They soon returned with weapons and proceeded to clean and load their pieces. Preparations completed, they stuffed extra rounds in their pockets, kissed the womenfolk, and headed for the door. I looked longingly at Bob, pleading with my eyes to be allowed to join their expedition. I'd gladly have carried a lantern, bullets, even bandages.

"Dad," Bob responded, "can Jack come?"

"Jack?" puzzled Dad McCoy, "why, he ain't none of us."

"He's my best friend," Bob insisted, while I shook my head rigorously in agreement.

Dad McCoy sized me up and down as he weighed the suggestion. Like an ancient patriarch he stroked his beard with a callused hand as I stood trembling with hope.

"Hmmm, it sure would smart their minds knowing they was shot on by a Pollock," he chuckled, "and just about what they deserves."

A rifle was thrust into my arms and I crushed it to my chest. I was so filled with gratitude that I could only offer complete silence to express my feelings. We marched out to the barn to saddle the horses for Dad McCoy insisted upon an old-fashioned attack.

"Where's the horses?" Dad McCoy thundered as we viewed the rows of empty stalls.

"I told Don to get them," Dave explained.

"I had to milk so I asked Bob to fetch them," Don quickly replied.

"Mom asked me to chop wood and I told Betty to bring them," was Bob's defense.

"Tarnation and bullfrogs!" roared Dad McCoy, "ain't no way we can catch those critters in the dark. Just pure luck for them Hatfields, but, there'll be another time, just you count on that."

With his promise of a future foray to comfort us, we hurried back to the house and loudly blamed the women for ruining our evening. They soon won forgiveness with a feast of hot corn bread, fried chicken, and cold buttermilk. For dessert, Dad McCoy ran off a string of yarns about those horrible Hatfields and magnificent McCoys that lasted until midnight.

Several years elapsed before I became aware of just how deftly they had pulled my leg without working up a scent of suspicion. I was amazed, but gratified, at the time and effort they took to pull their prank on one little Pole. It confirmed my belief that the McCoys considered me one of their very own. As far as I was concerned, whatever joke had been perpetrated was purely on the Hatfields.

Discipline Principles

Effective discipline requires loyalty and a sense of belonging.

A strong organization exacts leadership, and leadership demands discipline. God designed and Moses followed this chain–of–command system: "So I took the heads of your tribes, wise and experienced men, and appointed them heads over you, leaders of thousands, and of hundreds, of fifties and of tens, and officers for your tribes" (*Deuteronomy 1:15, NASB*).

Discipline Practices

While discipline begins at home it is also modified and enhanced by schools, churches, sports, jobs, clubs, and your neighbors. These experiences out of the home can be helpful or harmful depending upon the individual situation.

Good discipline is achieved and maintained in organizations like the Boy Scouts, Girl Scouts, Pioneer Girls, AWANA, 4-H, etc., because they help satisfy these basic needs:

- A person must feel wanted and needed by a group.

- The group and its goals must be important and meaningful to the individual.

- A person wants to identify with the group and make a personal contribution to its success.

- The group is active in various interesting activities.

- The leaders are genuinely interested in a joiner.

Encourage and guide your child into joining those groups which will help develop a good attitude toward discipline.

Neighbors, friends, and even relatives can often accomplish things with children that their parents seem unable to attain. For some strange but providential purpose, parents do not hold the entire destiny of their children. It is a wise parent who seeks the services of friends to complete his child's training.

Discipline Proverbs

- It is more profitable to be a participant than a parasite.

- To be something means to belong to someone.

- "A mirror reflects a man's face, but what he is really like is shown by the kind of friends he chooses" (*Proverbs 27:19, LB*).

10. The Fourth of July Race

"All boys for the 50 yard dash report to the start-ing line," echoed the announcer's voice from the public address system.

It was the annual Fourth of July celebration at the Lewis and Clark State Park. Families had traveled for miles around to enjoy this full day of food, festivities, and fireworks. Mother and Daddy Pete's return from Texas in time for this occasion added to my happiness.

I left the amazing sights and sounds of the men's pie-eating contest and headed for the dirt track. The 50 yard dash was for boys in grades one to three of the local schools. I had the honor to repre-sent Baker School and a chance to win the prize of a new silver dollar.

We lined up as the crowd collected along the track to cheer for their home school. The starter gave his final instructions and then began his countdown. The pistol cracked and we leaped to the challenge. I had a fast break and led all the way, winning by several yards.

The announcer asked my name and school and presented me with a silver dollar amid the cheers from the Baker School crowd. My easy victory must have awakened some suspicion in the announcer's mind.

"Are you in the third grade?" he asked.

"Yes," I answered truthfully.

"You're kind of big," he quizzed, "just how old are you?"

"Nine," I replied.

"Nine years," he gasped, "and still in the third grade?"

"I missed a year of school in Florida," I explained. He mumbled something about "those Southerners" as I scampered to my mother.

"Mommie," I asked, "will you keep this dollar for me so I won't lose it?"

She gave me a bear hug and buried the dollar in her purse. I stood proudly by her side to watch the 75 yard dash by the fourth through sixth graders. After calling them to the line, the announcer blared out, "Where's that skinny kid who won the first race? Maybe he'd like to try his chances against boys his own age?"

Mother shoved me onto the track where the Baker School group made my presence painfully aware. The announcer asked for silence. "O.K., boy," he chuckled, "get down to the starting line. I just hope you're as good a loser as you were a winner."

The novelty of a third grader in this race attracted a larger crowd. The starter gave the same set of instructions and countdown. The pistol exploded and so did I. My bolting to the lead aroused a roar of approval from the multitude who knew a good thing when they saw it. Their cheers quickly digressed to laughter which must have had a demoralizing effect on the bigger boys.

The spectators were not laughing at the sight of bigger boys being beaten, but at my peculiar running style. I was helplessly and hopelessly pigeon-toed in both feet. The poor people simply couldn't comprehend how my turned-in-toes were evading each other's company. By every law of physics I should have tripped over myself, or at the very least suffered some self-inflicted wounds. Their uproarious encouragement gave me the racer's edge, and I again flashed across the finish line first.

For the second time the announcer went through the formality of mentioning my name and school. As he handed me the silver dollar, he growled, "Kid, you sure are lucky."

Mother gave me a second bear hug, more encompassing than the first, and hid the second silver dollar in her purse. Friends clustered round to congratulate, while strangers came to inspect my legs to see if everything was orthodox. I could now watch the 100 yard dash of the seventh and eighth graders in safety and dignity.

The announcer called the last race and the big boys pranced to the line where they flexed their hairy muscles that I envied.

"Hey," sang out the announcer, "where's that pigeon-toed kid from Baker School?"

A hundred voices roared; a hundred hands pointed in my direction. I tried to duck behind my mother, but she refused to cooperate.

"How'd you people like to see the kid take on some real competition?" the announcer suggested. The response was positively deafening and disgraceful, resembling the approval that must have greeted Christians in the Coliseum. I *froze*. Mother clutched me by the shoulders and whispered, "I know you're tired."

Tired! The physical exhaustion and mental excitement of winning two races had drained me to the dregs.

"It's not fair to ask you to run again," she continued. "I don't care if you win, but you'd make me very proud if you tried."

For mother I'd have run over broken glass on my knees and elbows. I couldn't speak, I could only nod my consent. A tremendous cheer went up as mother walked with me to the starting line.

Word spread like wildfire throughout the park, causing all other activities to cease. This delay, to allow the crowd to gather at the track, gave me a chance to catch my breath. Unknown hands reached out to pat me, strange faces spoke words of encouragement; but I only had eyes and ears for mother. She sensed my deep despair, the dread of defeat after so much victory, and she continued to reassure and relax me.

"They're rooting for you," she said softly, pointing to the people. I nodded, too filled with fear to attempt words. We reached the starting line where the bigger boys had been waiting and watching our approach. As I stood beside them and viewed their size, my courage shriveled. At this low tide of confidence, mother put starch in my stature.

"Give me your tennis shoes," she whispered. "I want you to run barefooted, just like an Indian."

Running barefooted was my usual mode of travel and the soles of both feet had the calluses to prove it. But bare feet were a symbol of poverty, and at a Fourth of July celebration I didn't want the world to know that we were *that* poor. Still, running like an Indian had a nice patriotic ring to it, and it fired my imagination. I yanked off both shoes and gave them to mother.

It was a gimmick, my mother's ultimate weapon for her only son. Taking off my shoes in public was an open challenge that I meant business—just like when a man rolls up his sleeves and spits on his hands. It made me feel good. My feet, no longer encumbered with canvas, felt free and natural as they caressed the soft earth.

The psychological effect on the bigger boys was devastating! They must have longed to shuck their shoes and run feet–free, but it was too late. To remove their shoes now would only admit to fear, or even worse, the accusation of becoming a copy cat.

Mother gave me a tender hug. "Yennie," she whispered, using her sweetest way of saying Jack in Polish, "I'm going to wait for you at the finish line. Promise me that when you run you won't look back or down. Hold your head high and look only at me."

I promised.

The announcer walked up and spoke to a tall boy on the line. "Son," he warned, "don't let the Baker kid beat you!"

The starter began his opening lecture which I could now repeat verbatim. He walked down the line, moving back those who had fudged past the line scratched on the ground. He paused to examine my bare feet, then slipped me a fast wink that seemed to say, "Go get 'em!"

Toes hooked in the earth, I leaned forward as the countdown began. The gun fired, the crowd erupted, and I catapulted into the lead. Faster and faster I drove my freed feet into the dirt, using each toe as a springboard. This time my head was up, as mother instructed, looking straight at her. It was almost mystical, so dreamlike, I could see the crowd but I couldn't hear them. The only sounds that were real was mother's voice in front and the bigger boys catching up to me from behind.

I ran, but the longer distance tore at my strength and the bigger boys gained ground and confidence. I could hear mother's voice, "Yennie ... Yennie ... my Yennie!" A big boy pulled alongside as we drove for the finish line. We matched stride for stride but with longer legs the advantage was his. Then mother's voice reached out, like hands, and pulled me toward her. With every ounce of energy I flung myself forward in one final frenzy and fell into her tender arms.

It was over. I had done my very best, and so had mother. I buried my head on her breast, too tired to care, too happy to know. The crowd became silent as the judges huddled to determine whose body, or portion thereof, had crossed the finish line first. I clung to mother, sensing her pride as she praised, "Yennie, you did so good, so very good."

The judges arrived at their decision and gave it to the announcer. He cleared his throat. "The winner of the 100 yard dash is—" he took full advantage of his position and paused to adjust his glasses, "that kid from Baker School."

The crowd roared their approval. The Baker School group went wild with jubilation while our Polish clan was so excited that they hurled Polish phrases to the startled spectators. Mother squeezed me so tightly that my toes curled. I was no longer capable of standing or understanding. There is a limit to the amount of happiness a small boy can contain.

After several minutes of pleading the announcer restored some semblance of order and requested my presence to receive the silver dollar. I managed to trot to the microphone as the crowd applauded.

"The winner of the 100 yard dash from Baker School, is—" the announcer paused, leaned over, and asked me my name. I gave it gladly. The crowd whistled and cheered as I reached for the silver dollar, which the announcer offered, but before I could grasp it, he flipped it into the dust.

I was shocked, but the crowd was infuriated! A round of rather lusty and hot "Boos!" expressed their sentiments for his display of poor sportsmanship. The announcer must have been stung to shame, or maybe he overheard Dad McCoy's cold opinion of what should be done to "worthless varmints." He bent over to retrieve the coin, but my hand was quicker than his repentance. I snatched it up and walked back to mother.

The rest of the afternoon I devoted to sitting upon my laurels. Just about everyone in the Baker School District sought me out to shake my hand. It was heady stuff, and I purely enjoyed it. Fortunately, some of the bigger boys from the race came over to extend their congratulations. This praise from my peers had a wholesome humbling effect as they taught me what being a good loser really means.

Picnic over, we loaded up our trusty Model A's and headed for home. I had recovered sufficiently to begin some thoughts on how to spend my fortune. I felt a deep need to share it with the family. Mother's instruction to run like an Indian recalled an ad I had seen in the local newspaper. The evening was young and I decided to treat the entire family to see the frontier classic by James Fenimore Cooper, *Last of the Mohicans* starring Gary Cooper.

We hurried home, changed into our town clothes, and then left for Vancouver, Washington. My three dollars paid for the gasoline, tickets, popcorn, and ice cream sodas for two car loads of happy Poles. True, it was during the Great Depression, and money did go a lot further than it does now; but back in those days you had to go a lot further for the money.

Discipline Principles

A child's first source of inspiration and encouragement is his parents. No one—child, youth, or adult—ever outgrows his need of parents.

Discipline Practices

The child's character, personality, and discipline begins at home. No other institution can replace the home and parents when it comes to raising and training children. Children receive their head start in life at home, not in a school, not even in the church. Parents should be the child's first counselor, the one they look to for strength and guidance.

Young man, obey your father and your mother. Tie their instructions around your finger so you won't forget. Take to heart all of their advice. Every day and all night long their counsel will lead you and save you from harm; when you wake up in the morning, let their instructions guide you into the new day. For their advice is a beam of light directed into the dark corners of your mind to warn you of danger and to give you a good life (*Proverbs 6:20–23, LB*).

Children need to be praised, to know that their parents are really proud of them. There are several areas in which parental pride is appropriate.

■ Parents should be proud of their child's accomplishments.

■ Even when a child apparently fails, parents can still be proud that he tried.

■ Above and beyond what a child does or doesn't, parents should be proud for the child, himself. Every child is valuable and worthy of our praise and pride.

Discipline Proverbs

■ If parents don't understand, try grandparents.

■ A little praise earns a lot of interest.

■ Unearned praise outweighs earnest criticism.

■ "Praise is becoming to the upright" *(Psalm 33:1, NASB).*

11. Bully for You

"Klunkers" is an ancient game, probably dating back to the chariots of Egypt. It was a favorite at Baker School, since we could play it while eating lunch. When dismissed, we raced for position. The "King" sat under the quince tree, followed by his court. The last person in line was the "Klunker."

The object of the game was to watch the cars go by and rate them as to value. Our school overlooked the highway between Vancouver and Seattle, so there was ample traffic to supply our needs. It was like a spelldown, those getting the better cars moved toward the King; while those with the jalopies moved down the line toward the Klunker. With a lot of luck it was possible for a Klunker to become King, providing the traffic cooperated.

Decisions were made by common consent and usually followed this pattern: tractors were better than wagons, trucks were better than tractors, cars were better than trucks, and Greyhound buses were the best of all! Naturally, new was better than old, and Buicks were better than Fords. When no common agreement was possible, the King gave the final verdict.

Ron, a new boy at school, used a game of Klunkers to dethrone me from my position in Mrs. Lambert's room. Ron had only been at school for a couple of weeks, but that was sufficient time for all the boys to dislike him. There were several reasons for our prejudice. First, he was the biggest boy in the room, and size alone is worthy of suspicion. Second, he had a pug nose, which the boys considered infuriatingly masculine. Finally, he came from Portland, Oregon, which made him a foreigner and a city–slicker.

It was probably Ron's loneliness, and a desire to win friends, that goaded him into action. I was King of the Klunker game and had to decide between Ron's Cadillac and Freckles' Buick. Ron voiced his disapproval of my judgment.

"What did you say?" I demanded, rising to my feet.

"I said," Ron repeated, "that my Klunker was better."

"But I said it wasn't!" I shot back.

"Then you better get glasses!" Ron replied.

Glasses! That was the one insult no one could laugh off or ignore. I broke a twig from the quince tree and placed it on my left shoulder.

"That twig says I'm right," I challenged.

Ron rose to his feet, near the end of the line, and marched up to place himself at my disposal.

"That twig says you're wrong," he retorted, and flicked the twig off my shoulder with his right hand. Naturally, my eyes followed the falling twig, so I did not notice Ron's left hand. It crashed into my face like a twelve gauge shotgun! The twig and I reached the ground about the same time. Blood spurted from my swollen nose. Loyal friends quickly lifted me to my feet, even before I had time to comprehend this assault in broad daylight.

"Cheating city–slicker," they hissed. "You didn't square off first!"

By every rule held honorable, Ron had violated the very fiber of fighting ethics. After the twig had been twitted, the combatants were then allowed a few moments to flex muscles and demonstrate their talents by shadowboxing. Everybody knew that. Even the French allowed a few introductory swipes with the rapier before serious slicing.

"We stopped squaring off in Portland years ago," Ron protested.

"You're in the country now," Bob McCoy answered.

"Go back to Portland!" Freckles added, as he wiped the blood off my chin.

"O.K., I'm sorry," Ron apologized. "We'll square off."

Square off we did, and I took plenty of time to flush the butterflies out of my brain. During this delay I noted Ron's muscular development and his above average skill in shadowboxing. I was impressed.

Preliminaries completed, the boys formed a circle of bodies about us. We faced, exchanged mutual nods, and Ron moved in like a thrashing machine, throwing haymakers in all directions. I cast boxing to the breeze, ducked under his flailing fists, and hit him with a flying tackle. Ron was unprepared for football and went down with a thud which left him breathless. While Ron gasped for breath, I flipped him on his side and encircled his stomach with my legs. I locked ankles in a classic scissors hold and started squeezing.

"Finish him off!" yelled Freckles.

"No hurry," I gloated. "Let's see what the city boy can do with my farm legs."

Ron struggled, but lack of oxygen rapidly drained away his strength. His cheeks turned pale with a bluish hue. I knew I had him.

"Here comes the teacher!" somebody shouted.

To be caught fighting meant a whipping by the principal and a note sent home which insured a second application. I unhooked my ankles, jumped up, and brushed the stains of battle off my clothes. Without a backward glance, I took off to hide behind the quince tree.

It was a false rumor. While I had been grooming in an attempt to establish an aura of innocence, Ron had staggered to his feet. He regained both breath and lust for revenge simultaneously. With no teacher present, the sight of my retreating body was more temptation than he could bear.

Ron attacked me from the rear and I fell forward with him firmly attached to my back. It was now my turn to feel the bereavement of breathlessness. I tried to rise, but his weight was more than I could muster. I attempted to roll, but his legs locked me firmly beneath his body. I was saddled with Ron and he proceeded to put the spurs to me.

"Ride 'em city slicker!" he yipped as he bounced upon my defenseless flesh. His left hand held me by the collar. With his right fist he pummeled all available parts of my body from Dan to Beersheba.

Freckles finally arrived and seeing my plight tried to help. "Lookout!" he warned, "Mrs. Lambert's coming!" But Ron's dedication to my education made him oblivious to this ruse. Mercifully, the school bell rang.

"Had enough?" asked Ron.

"Yah—ick," I mumbled, trying to speak with a mouth full of dirt and debris.

"Then say uncle," Ron ordered.

"Uncle," I blurted, relieved at how easy it was

to say that dreadful word.

Ron removed himself and swaggered off, the new bully supreme of Mrs. Lambert's room. He was surrounded by a host of admirers; how quickly they forgot my triumphs in football and the Fourth of July race. The faithful few helped me to my feet.

"You had him whipped," insisted Bob McCoy.

"It was a dirty trick, yelling teacher," cried Cousin Bob.

"He jumped you from behind," added Freckles. "When you going to fight him again?"

"Only if he catches me," I sighed, "and by then he'll be too tired to do anything."

Prior to this time, Freckles and I had never been too friendly. My public humiliation somehow drew us together and Freckles joined my small circle of trusted friends. Blood, apparently, is not only thicker than water, it's stickier.

During the summer, Ron grew several inches and added more pounds to his frame. I realized how lucky I had been in fighting and losing to the smaller model. Even more fortunate, the defeat left a sour taste for combat. In the future I would rely on words, logic, humor, friendship, love, and finally full flight as a substitute for violence. From personal experience I knew that anything is less painful than the bottom position of a brawl.

Discipline Principles

Troubles, depending on how we react, either draw us closer together or drive us farther apart. "A friend loveth at all times, and a brother is born for adversity" (*Proverbs 17:17*).

Discipline that is based on force is both poorly instilled and weakly maintained. Force generates fear and results in resentment. "There is no fear in love; but perfect love casteth out fear: because fear hath torment ..." (*1 John 4:18*).

Discipline Practices

Every group, from church choirs to criminals, depends on rules to live by. Children, in their games and activities, desire regulations and referees to enforce them. Parents can explain to their children that the family needs the same type of laws children use on their peers.

Children readily learn from nature that you don't disturb hornets or tease cats that are Siamese. Solomon put it this way: "He that passeth by, and meddleth with strife belonging not to him, is like one that taketh a dog by the ears" (*Proverbs 26:17*). Children should be encouraged to give the same consideration and respect to people that they have for animals.

Discipline Proverbs

- Happiness is being on vacation when trouble comes calling.

- Friends stick with you, but foes just stick you.

- Life is jammed with stale bread.

- "There are friends who lead one to ruin, others are closer than a brother" (*Proverbs 18:24, The Jerusalem Bible*).

12. Heaven or Help

"Jack!" Cousin Bob cried, "Mr. Sture's coming!"

We both stopped chopping weeds and watched his ancient Model A chug up the driveway and stop at the house.

"Get to work," Uncle Joe ordered. "You're not out here to watch cars."

"But Uncle Joe," I explained, "Mr. Sture has come to hear me say my Bible verses for the Sunday school contest, I'm going—" Uncle Joe glared at me and I automatically stopped talking and started hewing weeds.

"Sunday's the day for Bible," he concluded. "Today you work!"

Like a puppy, I tried begging with my eyes, but my maternal godfather was beyond approach. I watched in despair as Conrad Sture left his car and headed for us, blithely unaware of the situation. Uncle Joe saw him coming, and decided to meet him halfway. He dropped his hoe and hurried down the hill to intercept my hero.

Conrad Sture had fought in World War I and lost one of his lungs to poison gas. Unable to do physical work, he devoted his bachelor years to helping children. He was my Sunday school teacher and gave me the first book I ever owned, a leather bound New Testament.

Our Sunday school had set up a contest to see which child could learn the most Bible verses in a month. Conrad had encouraged me to enter and promised to help me with the chore of memorizing. It was for this purpose that he came to our farm on a Saturday afternoon, to find me working with the family in our corn field.

"Oh, boy," groaned Cousin Bob, "Mr. Sture's going to get it now."

I shook my head in agreement, knowing full well that my frail and meek Sunday school teacher was no match for Uncle Joe. They met in the pasture, out of listening range but their actions could be clearly seen. The conversation appeared to be heated from Uncle Joe's side of the argument. He waved his hands and stomped his boots like a man fighting bees and ants at the same time. Conrad just calmly stood there listening. I fully expected Mr. Sture to be picked up and deposited in his car. The debate suddenly ceased and Uncle Joe paced back to the corn patch.

"Jack," he commanded, "how many of those verses do you have to say?"

"About twenty."

"All right, you can go," he relented, "but not looking like that. Wash up and put on some clean clothes since you're going to be religious."

Conrad was already waiting in his car as I ran to the house and made myself presentable. With my New Testament and list of verses, I dashed to his car.

"Suppose we drive to Salmon Creek," he suggested. "We can park in the shade, and afterwards you might want to test the water."

I smiled happily at the thought of Salmon Creek on a hot afternoon. As we puttered down the gravel road, my curiosity blossomed into words.

"Mr. Sture," I asked, "what did you say to Uncle Joe?" If there were any magic words that worked on my uncle, I certainly wanted to know them. Like Simon the sorcerer, I was willing to buy the power (see *Acts 8:9–19*).

"I just asked," Conrad replied.

"Just asked?" I cried. "Didn't you say something special like?"

"Well, let's see," he mused. "Come to think of it, I did use a special word."

"What was it!" I begged.

"Please," laughed Conrad. "I did say, 'Please.'"

"And it worked?" I questioned.

"Just like magic," he answered.

We parked beside the creek, and I handed him my list of verses. Conrad opened his Bible and read off the first one. "John 11:35."

"Jesus wept," I answered proudly.

"I see you found the short ones," he chuckled, "but it still counts as a verse. Genesis 1:1."

So the afternoon went by as I repeated my verses, including the Lord's Prayer and the Ten Commandments. Conrad suggested that for my next memorization I work on entire chapters, such as Psalm 23, 1 Corinthians 13 and Ecclesiastes 12.

For the next month, Conrad came every Saturday afternoon to hear my Bible verses. He was my special hero and I really bent my mind to please him. I also appreciated being paroled from the corn field, and wading in Salmon Creek was a cool treat. At the end of the month I had mastered 362 verses according to Mr. Sture's official count. The girl who won second place had only 187.

In his quiet and meek way, Conrad was a tower of strength in Christ. He had that beautiful ability to love children under all conditions and circumstances. Having no children of his own, he adopted all of us. We loved him, not only for what he did for us, but for what he was.

Discipline Principles

Discipline becomes most disagreeable and difficult under conditions of anger. It is better to wait and allow tempers to cool than to press a heated issue. "A gentle answer turns away wrath, but a harsh word stirs up anger" (*Proverbs 15:1, NASB*).

Children, especially the younger ones, are very susceptible to adult influence. Their tendency to "hero worship" teachers, grandparents, and special neighbors can complicate or complement parental authority.

Discipline Practices

Every community has its Conrad Stures and Dad McCoys to assist parents in raising their children. For example, Conrad was a bachelor with no experience in raising his own children. But he knew, loved, and helped children. The beauty of bachelorhood is that it affords much free time to spend on children. Since Conrad was a Christian, he was able to strengthen me spiritually. Childless couples are another source of unspent love for children.

Discipline Proverbs

- If you must pour cold water on a person, pour it on his anger.

- Help a boy and you have a friend; love a boy and you have a son.
- To remain young associate with young people.
- Fair words becalm the barks of strife.

13. Teacher Crush

Daddy Pete found a job in Portland and we moved to a house of our own in Scholls, Oregon. I shed some sadness over leaving my grandparents, Conrad Sture, Baker School, and those McCoys.

My new school was a one room affair with all eight grades within four stout walls. A large wood heater in the back of the room provided heat, work assignments, and entertaining sound effects. Miss Brown, the teacher, was small, young, pretty, and fresh out of college.

Discipline was different under Miss Brown. Since all the boys fell madly in love with her, she only had to hint and we obeyed. The flicker of her long eyelashes carried more authority than a yardstick's swat. The sweet smell of her perfume tranquilized us. Just to be smiled on by Miss Brown was worth any sacrifice. She captivated the bigger boys, and they made sure the smaller students gave her no cause for concern.

At the end of the second week of school, Miss Brown announced her feelings for me. "Jack," she asked, "how would you like to be in the fifth grade?"

"Fifth grade?" I questioned, wondering what would happen to the fourth grade I now resided in.

"I've checked your card, and you're old

enough," she replied. "I believe you can do fifth grade work. You'd make me very happy if you tried."

To make Miss Brown happy I'd have leaped into the eighth grade and thrown in some high school classes for good measure. Since I was the only fourth grade student, my promotion did reduce her teaching load, and this might have been her main motive. This unexpected promotion was like being knighted, and my coronation took place before the entire school. I was moved from the last desk in the fourth grade row to the first position in the fifth grade row. My new desk was the closest one in the room to Miss Brown.

"I'm giving Jack the front desk," she explained, "so that he'll be near me for special help now that he has skipped a grade."

The students accepted her decision in silence, filled with envy at my exaltation. It seemed impossible that a new boy at school could be skipped a grade, assigned the best desk, and promised special attention by Miss Brown all in one day. My cup overflowed and spilled on others! Clyde, the biggest boy, became insanely jealous of such familiarities with his lady love. Since he lacked the intelligence to express his madness in words, he resorted to action. My only defense was to flee; my only offense was a choice vocabulary. Clyde finally managed to corner me one day and dragged me into the schoolhouse.

"Miss Brown, Jack cursed me," he tattled.

"He what?" she gasped.

"Yes'm," squealed Clyde. "He truly swore on me!"

"What did he say?" she inquired, rather

timidly.

"Oh, I can't repeat that to you," Clyde lied, "but I can write it out."

He found a scrap of paper and began his composition. Clyde wasn't anything special at spelling, and some of my expressions forced him to sweat over his penmanship. When he was finally satisfied, he gave Miss Brown a loose translation. She read, winced, and even placed a dainty hand over her mouth to stifle a sigh. I was in such anguish watching her reactions that I ached to the ankles.

"Jack," she finally spoke, "did you actually say this?"

I took the paper from her outstretched hand. Clyde's scrawlings were difficult to decipher, even though I knew what he was trying to repeat. Most of his words were pretty well crippled up; a few were downright decapitated. Yet, in spite of his spelling, he had pretty well managed to express the depths of my vulgar sediments.

"Yes, Miss Brown," I confessed, "that's about what I said."

"I'm shocked," she sorrowed, "and deeply disappointed in you. Jack, how could you be so *naughty*?"

The way she said "naughty," and wrinkled her nose, made me feel filthy.

"What am I going to do with you?" she wailed.

I stood in dumb despair, trying to concoct a scourging worthy of my crime. I almost suggested she wash my mouth with Fels Naphtha or Drain-O, but neither seemed caustic enough.

"I cannot allow myself to associate with such conduct," she sniffed. "You will now sit at the end of the row."

End of the row! It was the end of the world, banishment from her immediate presence and affection. The moment school was out I sprinted home, hoping to escape the jeers of my peers.

I was safely resting on our front lawn when Clyde strolled by. He seized this opportunity to ridicule my new seating arrangement at school. The sight and sound of this bully inflamed me. At home, on my own land, and protected by the Bill of Rights, I exercised freedom of speech. I blistered Clyde's ears to a purple perfection. Happily, I gained the door before the rocks struck. Behind the safety of the front window I flashed a few faces which reduced Clyde to a towering rage.

Clyde ran home and wrote out a full account of my latest transgressions. These he presented promptly, the following morning, for Miss Brown's education. She read and reread his glowing descriptions before calling me to her judgment desk.

"Jack, did you call Clyde these things after school, yesterday?" she asked, "and make faces at him?"

I had no intention of denying these accomplishments and freely admitted to a job well done.

"How could you?" she demanded, with a tone of sternness.

"But I didn't do it at school, Miss Brown," I cried. "I was at home when it happened."

"That makes absolutely no difference!" she snapped. "The truth is you used foul language and grotesque faces."

I was confused. Miss Brown had no right to rule me at home; that was my mother's job. As for Clyde, he was on a public road over which teachers have no jurisdiction.

"But, Miss Brown—" I tried to explain the legal

loophole, but she cut me off short.

"Since you will not be persuaded by other means, I have no other choice," she pronounced. "You have forced me to whip you."

A wave of awe rippled over the students. Miss Brown had never whipped a child, at least not at school. I was about to be her solo spanking experience. Miss Brown grasped the rod and faced me.

"Bend over!" she ordered.

I dropped my head and seized both legs in the "penalty posture" used at Baker School. This position had the advantages of providing an ample target and allowing the victim to pinch his legs. Through some happy accident we had discovered that fingernail acupuncture of the limbs helped deaden the pains of the posterior. Miss Brown hesitated, uncertain as to the best course of approach. She finally threw back her arm in grim determination and let fly the rod.

It was awful!

I had braced myself for a horsewhipping, vowing not to beg, cry, or to be knocked to the floor. Her first blow was beyond anything I had ever experienced or expected. It was so slow and fragile that it failed to sting; worse yet, the sound it produced was insensitive. Instead of a noble *"Thawack!"* all that ensued was a feeble *"thip."*

I had been insulted! All was lost as her love taps destroyed the last rights of the condemned:

- The right to swift and proper punishment;

- The right to remain silent as evidence of your manhood, thereby earning admiration from the spectators;

- The right to invoke sympathy from those same

spectators should you be brought to tears.

Miss Brown's blows were neither swift, sure nor grounds on which I could capture the admiration or empathy of my peers. I bit my knee to keep from laughing. The class, free from such obligation, laughed for me and at me. Confused at their barbaric delight, Miss Brown quickly concluded the exercise.

"There!" she exclaimed proudly, "that should teach you to be good. You may return to your desk."

I arose, slunk back to my desk, and slouched down to escape as much humiliation as possible. I knew what my classmates were thinking, for I had come to the same conclusion: Miss Brown didn't care enough to give me a decent whipping. Her indifference to my needs was inexcusable. She had now torn from my heart whatever shreds of puppy love had lingered. I now looked upon Miss Brown as a teacher, simply that and nothing more or less.

Discipline Principles

Effective discipline requires the generous application of love and firmness, in the proper proportions, for each individual child and circumstance. There is no conflict between love and firmness. Problems are created when man attempts to "put asunder" what God, human nature, and common sense "hath joined together."

Discipline Practices

Love cannot be bound or limited as to its manner of expression. To say "No," may reveal as much affection as to say, "Yes." A spanking can expose as much love as a kiss. Some will disagree, but then they've never been punished by my mother or kissed by Judas.

Being permissive will not guarantee that your child will love or even respect you. King David had many sons, but his favorite was Absalom. David indulged his son and the result was tragic. Absalom lost both love and respect for David. He died in his attempt to kill his own father so that he might become king (see *2 Samuel 15–18*).

Bribery and intimidation are weak substitutes for love and firmness. You cannot buy love from a child, neither can you frighten it out of him.

Love and firmness are not always on a fifty–fifty percentage. Children and circumstances vary in their needs and at times will require more of one than of the other.

A lack of firmness may be interpreted by the child as a lack of love and concern. This uncertainty may cause the child to push you to respond.

Discipline Proverbs

- Discipline is a combination of affection and correction.

- Baling the breeze and beating the air, such is the person who doesn't really care.

- "For when he punishes you, it proves that he loves you. When he whips you it proves you are really his child" (*Hebrews 12:6, LB*).

- "If you are churlish and arrogant and fond of filthy talk, hold your tongue; for wringing out the milk produces curd and wringing the nose produces blood, so provocation leads to strife" (*Proverbs 30:32, 33, NEB*).

14. 666 at Midnight

"Children," Miss Brown called us from our studies, "I have a special surprise for each of you." To our delight she held up a large package. "Who would like to guess what's inside?"

"Is it candy?" I shouted.

"No, Jack," she answered, "there are some things more important than candy."

"Is it crayons?" suggested Dorothy, the smartest girl in school.

"That's an excellent guess," praised Miss Brown, "but it's not crayons. It's something round and good for your health."

That caused a rash of answers from cough drops to bubble gum, but no matter how we twisted and pried, the riddle of the box remained a mystery.

"All right," Miss Brown remarked, "I'll show you a little bit of what they are." She opened the box carefully, like it was a carton of rattlesnake eggs, withdrawing a small round metal can.

"Shoe polish?" I blurted out.

"Oh, no," she laughed, "it's much nicer than shoe polish."

After another round of wild guesses, we all gave up. She waited until we were quiet and then proudly announced, "It's salve."

"Salve?" we chorused in dismay.

"Yes, cold salve," she explained. "There have been so many colds this winter that the school board purchased a can of cold salve for each student. Wasn't that thoughtful of them?"

"How does it smell?" inquired Jane.

"I'm not sure," Miss Brown replied. "Let's see." She twisted off the lid. "Well, it's medicine, but then you don't kill germs with perfume."

Assured that we wouldn't smell like lilacs, the boys were first in line to receive the school board's benevolence. Even if the ointment smelled obnoxious, it might keep mosquitoes away next summer.

At bedtime, mother carefully read the instructions and then coated me on the legs, chest, arms, and head. It had the consistency of axle grease blended with rancid lard. The scent was pungent enough to discourage the most desperate of germs. Feeling like a greased pig, I slipped under the covers. My body heat soon had the blankets reeking with menthol, Eucalyptus, and traces of horse liniment.

I awoke in a hot sweat, which I attributed to the salve, but I had no explanation for the cold chill in my heart. I felt strange, unreal, something was dreadfully wrong. "I'm dead," flashed the thought before I could control it. A quick pinch produced pain and the hope of life. "Maybe I'm dying?" was the next terrible conclusion. I fumbled for the flashlight and inspected my body with its beam. Everything seemed there and appeared to be operational, yet the apprehension of danger persisted.

"It must be the salve," I wondered. "There's something in it that is making me sick." I scrambled out of bed and picked up the can. By the pale gleam of the flashlight I checked the contents. Then the dawn thundered across my mind as I noticed the trademark for the first time. There, in large red numerals, blazed the unholy horror of "666".

"Oh, no!" I gasped, "it's the Mark of the Beast!" I recalled reading the book of the Revelation in the New Testament Conrad Sture had given me. I had never read such painful descriptions of devils, monsters, and the punishment of the wicked. The Four Horsemen, the Seven Last Plagues, and the Lake of Fire burned holes in my imagination. I came out of Revelation with one great determination: under no circumstance would I allow the Beast to brand the mysterious "666" in my hand or forehead (see *Revelation 13:11–18*).

"The Mark of the Beast!" I repeated in terror as I dropped the can of salve in horror. I checked my palms with the flashlight to see if the lethal numbers had been etched in my skin. I was relieved to find both hands brandless. I then felt my forehead to see if any swelling or indentation had begun.

"Is there still time?" I questioned. The clock showed five minutes to midnight. "Midnight!" I tried to think. "That's when the devil comes to claim your soul. If this 666 salve is on me, I'm a goner!"

There was only one desperate chance—the devilish ointment had to be removed before Lucifer arrived. I dashed to the bathroom and concentrated on my hands and head, distinctly recalling from Revelation that those were the locations to be marked. First I used alcohol to remove all excess satanic salve from my skin. While I rubbed, I prayed, asking the Lord to save me from my sins in general and the devil in particular.

"How could I be so stupid?" I berated myself. "How could I even touch a can with 666 on it, after having read Revelation?" I was also shocked that my own dear mother had been the devil's tool to rub his brew into my hide. "How could mother do this to me?" I wailed as I washed.

I checked my forehead in the mirror, all seemed clean, but what about the salve that had penetrated my skin? Only moments were left, and I used them to advantage. A can of Old Dutch cleanser stood on the counter. I seized it, sprinkled the white powder on a brush, and then scoured both hands. Certain that my hands were decontaminated, I approached my forehead. The brush was loaded again, and I placed it to my skin, closed both eyes, and scrubbed! Foam, dirt, and skin flaked off my brow. Mother, awakened by these abnormal night sounds, investigated the bathroom. She caught me in the very act of saving my soul as she burst upon my baptism by brimstone.

"Jack! What are you doing?" she cried.

"Huh?" was my shocked response to her unexpected presence. I turned away so that she could not see my face.

"Have you been smoking?" she asked.

"No, Momma," I assured her. I grabbed a toothbrush. "I just wanted to brush."

"At midnight?" she demanded, rather suspicious.

I jammed the brush into my mouth to avoid answering.

"Turn around and face me when I talk to you," mother commanded.

There was no way out and I could think of nothing to say. I turned.

"Yennie!" she screamed, "you're bleeding!"

I stood there, with a face that felt like it had been kissed by barbed wire. I was too grown to cry and too small to explain. Mother immediately did to me what all mothers have done under such conditions: first aid, first; explanations, later.

"Haven't I told you a hundred times not to pick those pimples," she chided. "You want to end up with boils?"

"No, Momma," I could honestly answer. I saw no reason to correct her understanding as to my bleeding. How does one tell mother that she almost sold your soul to the devil? She gently washed my brow with cold water. "There, it has stopped bleeding," she comforted. "You'd better get to bed." She gave me a kiss and I left.

One final task remained before sleep was possible. Carefully, I picked up the can of salve and crept outside. There, under a sky full of stars, I flung it over the fence onto the neighbor's property, in the general direction of his pig pen. Should the devil desire his own, he'd know where to find it.

The next few days were filled with anxiety. I checked the mirror constantly, to see if I had been washed clean. I promised the Lord that under no condition would I ever have anything to do with "666" in any shape or form, not even if it came out as a candy bar.

Discipline Principles

The worst fear is fear of the unknown for it is based upon ignorance.

Children change, for better or for worse, but children change. This is a basic law of discipline and child training.

There are situations when it is best not to explain, but to keep silent. Solomon spoke of these moments when he wrote: "To every thing there is a season, and a time to every purpose under the heaven ... a time to keep silence, and a time to speak" (*Ecclesiastes 3:1, 7*).

Discipline Practices

Children are influenced and changed by what they see and hear. The Apostle Paul writes that by beholding we become changed (*2 Corinthians 3:18*). Especially in the early formative years, when parents have more control, children should be guided in their reading, seeing, and hearing experiences.

The right to remain silent is a privilege guaranteed in the Bill of Rights. There are times when children should be allowed this same privilege, and not be forced to answer, "Why did you do it?"

Discipline Proverbs

- There is no depth to which ignorance will not sink.

- "Be not afraid of sudden fear, neither of the desolation of the wicked, when it cometh. For the Lord shall be thy confidence, and shall keep thy foot from being taken" (*Proverbs 3:25, 26*).

- "Keep sound wisdom and discretion .... Then shalt thou walk in thy way safely" (*Proverbs 3:21, 23*).

15. Mothers Love Lilacs

"Put your books away," Miss Brown instructed. "I want each one of you to make a card for Mother's Day."

Joyfully we closed our books and dug out scissors and crayons. Miss Brown gave each child a sheet of construction paper, and our labor of love began. The next Sunday morning, before church, I gave my card to mother with a hug and a kiss.

Sunday afternoon I decided to surprise mother with a handful of wildflowers. I set off down the gravel road toward the Ryan farm. The Ryans were old people and kept to themselves. They had a mean hound dog to keep kids off the property, and he was known to carry his duties out onto the road. I picked up a hefty rock, just in case their dog decided to test me. As I neared their driveway, I noticed two large lilac bushes in the front yard. They were ablaze with purples and whites, their fragrance filling the air. Holding the rock firmly, I went to the front door and knocked. After a brief delay, old Mrs. Ryan appeared and cracked the door open.

"We ain't buying," she snapped, "and I told you that afore."

"I'm not selling," I hastily explained. Prior to

this I had tried to sell the Ryans the *Saturday Evening Post* magazine for a nickel.

"Then why you here?" she asked.

"I'd like to work some chores for you," I answered.

"Work!" she cackled. "We ain't got no money to pay for work."

"I don't want money, ma'am, just some flowers."

"Flowers?" she questioned, with a new note of interest in her voice. "Now why would a grown boy want flowers?"

"I'd like some flowers for my mother," I appealed. "It's Mother's Day. I'll work real hard for some of your lilacs."

"That so?" she mused. "You must be them new folks down the road on the Walker place."

"Yes'm."

"Just you wait till I get my spectacles," she ordered. In a few moments Mrs. Ryan returned. Perched on her nose were a set of horn-rimmed glasses, and she had a large butcher knife in her hand.

"What's your name?" she asked.

"It's Jack."

"Well, Jack, I've never sold a flower in my life, and I ain't about to begin," she lectured. "But, I've given heaps of them away. You above taking a gift?"

"Oh, no, ma'am!" I exclaimed.

She led me to the lilacs and proceeded to load me up; first with purples, then whites, and then back to purples. In the midst of her harvesting, Mr. Ryan and his hound arrived.

"Sarah," he questioned, "what on earth are you doing?"

"Prunin' my lilacs," she laughed.

"Ain't time for prunin'," he protested.

"Best time of all," she insisted, "specially if a boy's to make his mom happy on Mother's Day."

It was Mr. Ryan's turn to laugh, and the hound's opportunity to give me a sniffing over. Mr. Ryan pitched right in and helped his wife with her lilac reaping. I was soon covered with blossoms.

"I can't hold any more," I apologized. Even with both arms fully extended, I failed to encompass Mrs. Ryan's idea of a proper Mother's Day bouquet.

"That ought to give mom an idea of your feelings," she agreed. "Just be certain to tell her how much I enjoyed giving them, and you tell your mom to come visit me."

"I sure will," I promised, "and, thanks for being so nice."

They escorted me safely to the road and turned me in the right direction. The lilacs were so dense that I could not see through their clustered glory.

"Watch those feet and follow the road," Mr. Ryan cautioned.

"I'll be careful," I vowed.

Down the road I strode, a giant bouquet with two legs attached. After a short distance, I stopped and glanced back. The Ryans were still standing in the road, watching me. They waved and I nodded my head in happiness. It was a beautiful sight to see the Ryans standing close together, holding hands.

The journey home was slow. I was grateful that no cars came by to dust up the lilacs. I reached the house, mounted the steps to the porch, and paused before the door. Mother had told me that as a little boy, I had picked a handful of weeds and given them to her. That offering I had proudly called, "fires." I decided to repeat the performance.

There was no way to hold the lilacs and knock, so I kicked the door as respectfully as possible. I heard footsteps and the door swung open. I gambled it was mother, and not dad, standing in the doorway.

"Fires, Mommie!" I cried.

"Yennie!" she screamed, "is that you?"

"Fires!" I repeated for good measure.

Mother surged forward and clasped lilacs and me in a mighty hug.

"Don't crush the flowers," I gasped belatedly. My request went unheeded for mother was not to be denied her rights, especially on Mother's Day.

I can't really remember what mother enjoyed most—the lilacs, or my telling her how I came by them. One thing was certain, Mrs. Ryan's flowers sure made a lot of people happy on Mother's Day, whether they were mothers or not.

Discipline Principles

Some situations in life require the experience and expertise of the elderly. Life does not demand that you know all the answers, but you are expected to know someone who can help you.

Children who honor and respect the elderly are thrice blest: They gain honor; their parents are pleased and praised for having such noble children; and the elderly are awarded the considerations they so justly deserve.

Discipline Practices

Children should be guided and encouraged to seek help and counsel from the elderly. "Senior citizens" have the background, experience, and knowledge; the time and opportunity; and the desire and willingness.

Poverty is no excuse for neglecting to show our love and appreciation. Children should be shown by example the many ways in which they can express their feelings for others. Among these avenues of affection are personal projects and labors of love.

Nothing purchased can touch the heart as tenderly as something made with your very own hands. Children can make cards, bake bread, write letters, draw pictures. A child may be short on talent and hard pressed for ideas, but he can always work to express his feelings. Waxing dad's car and washing mother's windows, without being asked, are wonderful ways to say, "Thank you," and "I love you."

Discipline Proverbs

- Don't wait till the funeral to send flowers.

- Love is a special package, bound with a hug and sealed with a kiss.

- "An old man's grandchildren are his crowning glory ... " (*Proverbs 17:6, LB*).

- "Consider the lilies" (*Luke 12:27*).

16. So Long Silver

"Let's ride Silver," I suggested. It was a dull Sunday afternoon, and our band of rascals needed something to cure the boredoms.

"I'll get the apples," Bob McCoy chimed.

"And I can get some sugar," offered Freckles.

It was agreed, and with this tempting bait we headed for Mr. Long's pasture where Silver was quartered. Silver was a Percheron, that's French for "work horse." He was of majestic height and noble girth. His tremendous strength was exceeded only by his gentle disposition and addiction for sugar.

The secret to mounting Silver was to use a ladder or a stump. We never actually tried the ladder approach, probably because we had no imagination for its disposal once we were aboard. But there were plenty of stumps in the field for our ambitions. The trick was to maneuver Silver and berth him alongside a suitable stump. To coax him in the right direction we used apples, carrots, oats, and sugar cubes.

"I get to drive, since it was my idea," I informed my friends.

No one objected, and when Silver was positioned I clambered onto Silver's withers. The others followed with lots of puffing, shoving, and arguing while Bob McCoy stuffed Silver with apples.

"We're all on top," I shouted.

"I'll give him the sugar," Bob yelled.

Sugar was dessert, and once Silver tasted it, there was no holding him. Silver wouldn't budge without sugar, but upon receiving it he practically pranced for joy. Bob had to move fast in order to reach Silver's back before he lumbered off.

"Yippie!" we shouted, "Hi, ho, Silver!"

To encourage Silver to walk faster we attempted to spur him with our bare heels. This was an interesting impossibility from several viewpoints. First, our legs were too short to reach his flanks. Second, Silver's broad back extended out in all directions and forced our legs to do likewise. We didn't straddle Silver; we did the splits on him.

This style of riding made it difficult to remain aloft, since our legs could not clutch Silver's sides. Our only hold was to grasp the person in front tightly about the waist. The driver, at the end of the line, held Silver's cropped mane with both hands.

"Faster!" we cried, "the Indians are coming!"

Sometimes, if we bounced hard enough, Silver would speed things up to just a hint of a trot. Bouncing was fun, but tricky. Locked so tightly together, we had to synchronize our efforts with Silver and each other. When Silver decided the ride was over, he had his own style for removing the nuisance on his back. We all knew when that final moment arrived.

"Look out!" I warned. "He's heading for Sam's Hill!" Sam's Hill was the name we gave to a steep hillock near the center of the pasture.

"Turn him! Turn him!" yelled my comrades in arms.

Without benefit of bridle there was little I could do to deter Silver from this new direction.

Once Silver started his climb, the fate of the riders rested squarely upon the driver's grasp on Silver's mane. No team had ever made the top of Sam's Hill, but there was always the hope of victory.

"Hang on!" I shouted, as Silver started his climb.

"Don't let go!" my buddies encouraged.

Like an olympic toboggan team, we hunched, hugged, and hoped. The end always came the same way. A scream of anguish from the driver as Silver's short hairs slipped through his hands; a slight slippage of warning; and then the avalanche!

"Look out!" I shrieked, as Silver's mane left my hands. Firmly locked together we began our descent down Silver's back. Gathering momentum, we arched over his bottom and flew off into space, landing on the grass far below. No one ever was hurt, mainly because after impact we continued sliding backwards down the hill, like a skier off a high jump.

The moment his cargo broke loose, Silver stopped, until we were safely off his back. Then, and we always sat patiently for this final act, Silver would turn his massive head backwards and give us a careful looking over. I believe he was making sure we were all present and uninjured. Whatever Silver's purpose in perusing us, his dignified expression never failed to tickle our funny bones. At that look, we'd unlock bodies, and roll around in the grass with unashamed hilarity.

As for Silver, satisfied with our healthy disposition, he'd plod away to greener and quieter pasture.

Discipline Principles

The importance of nature study is clearly recommended in the Bible.

Take a lesson from the ants, you lazy fellow. Learn from their ways and be wise! For though they have no king to make them work, yet they labor hard all summer, gathering food for the winter *(Proverbs 6:6–8, LB)*.

But ask now the beasts, and they shall teach thee; and the fowls of the air, and they shall tell thee: or speak to the earth, and it shall teach thee: and the fishes of the sea shall declare unto thee *(Job 12:7, 8)*.

Discipline Practices

There are many ways in which children can learn discipline lessons from nature. Parents can relate personal experiences they have had with animals, tell and read animal stories to their children. Children can learn God's principles from reading the Bible and books on nature, watching television and films, and observing at the zoo.

Animals have their own rules and regulation to their life style. If followed, the barnyard runs smoothly. God has provided the tools in His Word for His highest creation—humans—to live a disciplined and beautiful life also.

Discipline Proverbs

- When humans act like animals, animals act like humans.

- Bees earn the respect of all men, because of their reward at each end.

17. Poor Pootsie

"Jack, did you remember to turn Pootsie loose?" Dad asked.

In the excitement of getting ready to leave for Portland, I had forgotten Dad's request to untie Pootsie, the family dog, a black and white terrier–type animal.

"No, Dad," I hedged, "I didn't want him running off while we were away and getting into trouble."

"I wish you had done what I told you," Dad replied.

"He'll be all right," I insisted. "There's plenty of food and water."

"And there's plenty of Gilmore, too," Dad sadly informed me.

Gilmore! I had neglected to take his hatred for Pootsie into account. Gilmore was king of the chickens, a huge Rhode Island Red rooster who ruled the roost. One of his recreations was to make Pootsie's life miserable, and he had the equipment to do it. Throughout the day, Gilmore chased Pootsie with a passion that somehow demonstrated the superiority of roosters over dogs. Pootsie's main refuge was the house, where roosters were not allowed to tread. However, if the door was closed, Pootsie scooted under the porch where he barked panickly to be rescued. Gilmore never followed him under the porch, even though there was room enough. Perhaps it was too confining for his leaping, spurring, and the final victory crowing.

"But the rope is long," I rationalized, "and Pootsie's faster than Gilmore."

"I guess he'll be all right," Dad comforted, "just as long as Gilmore doesn't circle him around that tree and shorten up the rope."

Dad's last remark ruined my day in Portland. Instead of enjoying the shopping trip, I longed to return home and save Pootsie. The picture of Gilmore stalking Pootsie around the tree haunted my mind.

Shopping over, we raced home. Before the car rolled to a stop in the driveway, I was out and running for the backyard. I heard Pootsie barking.

"He's alive!" I shouted back as I raced to the rescue. I rounded the corner of the house and saw Pootsie straining hard on the rope to get away from Gilmore. The rooster was dangerously close, and his mighty wings were outstretched wide in the attack position.

"Pootsie!" I screamed. "I'll save you!"

Pootsie yelped for joy as I dashed up, but Gilmore refused to move. "Gilmore!" I yelled, "get out or we'll have you for dinner!" I was shocked that my voice and approach had no effect on the rooster. He simply would not budge or behave! It was not until I reached Pootsie that I understood the cause for Gilmore's bravery; he was simply hung up on the job.

Somehow, during Pootsie's attempts to escape and Gilmore's leaping attacks, a loop of rope had snaked itself around the rooster's neck. At that opportune moment, Pootsie pulled hard on the rope to escape, and the tree held fast on the other end. Result: one shocked rooster strung up in the middle! To save himself, Gilmore stood on the tippy–tops of his talons and beat his wings on a take off attempt.

Dad arrived and together we freed Pootsie. With the tension on the rope gone, Gilmore flopped over in the grass, his usually scarlet head now a stale purple plum.

"Dad, is he dead?" I asked hopefully.

"His eyes are still blinking," Dad answered.

"Want me to get the axe?" I suggested.

"No," Dad replied, "let's see if he comes to."

We waited and watched while Gilmore collected his shattered strength and sanity. Finally, he reared up, teetered, tottered, and staggered for the chicken house. I followed, in the hope that he might still require the services of the axe.

Gilmore gained the chicken house and wobbled in. I peeked inside, just to make sure he was roosting all right. He wasn't roosting; instead, he had thrust himself headlong into the first empty nest, leaving his tail feathers drooping over the edge. Poor Gilmore, lack of oxygen must have caused some brain damage for him to seek refuge in accommodations designed for hens.

Even after a period of convalescence, Gilmore never forced his attentions upon Pootsie again. Whenever they chanced to meet, both developed an ingenious style for ignoring the opposition. Pootsie would start digging for a lost bone, while Gilmore chased invisible grasshoppers. In this back–to–back confrontation, both departed in dignity.

Discipline Principles

Animal pets afford the child an opportunity to develop responsibility and practice discipline in a very personal manner. Animals, depending on their degree of intelligence, take time to train their young. Those animals not trained, like turtles who hatch and head for the ocean, depend on instinct and mass births for survival. Among the higher forms of animals, like the bear, a long period of raising and training the young takes place. Both parents and children can learn valuable lessons of discipline by observing animals raise their young.

Children must be trained by their parents if they are to develop and mature. This means obeying even when opinions differ. "The rod and reproof give wisdom, but a child who gets his own way brings shame to his mother" (*Proverbs 29:15, NASB*).

Discipline Practices

Children learn valuable discipline lessons raising their own pets with parental guidance. Raising a pet, from a goldfish to a Saint Bernard, provides the opportunity to develop responsibility in a child. Specific duties for the care and comfort of the pet should be established:

- Feeding—proper food, at the right time, with the correct amounts
- Exercise on a daily basis, especially if the pet is confined or raised in the city
- Grooming
- Cleaning, both of the pet and its living quarters
- Training

Discipline goals and techniques become a very practical experience when the child helps in training the pet. Make a list of "Do's" and "Don'ts" with the child as to how the puppy should be trained:

Do's
- Come when called
- How to act on a leash
- How to act when tied up
- Perform certain tricks
- Be a watchdog and protect

Don'ts
- Use the rug for a bathroom
- Chew shoes, scratch furniture
- Bark constantly
- Jump on people
- Chase cats or cars
- Fight skunks or porcupines
- Eat food off the table

Explain and discuss with a child why it's important to train the puppy. Pets are appreciated and welcomed if they are well trained and behave themselves. Pets who are not trained, and who have bad manners, usually end up at the dog pound or are tied to a chain for safe keeping. A properly trained pet can be taken places with the family and not cause problems. A pet that obeys is a pet that can be trusted and enjoyed.

In dealing with their pets, children will gain insights and see relationships that explain the ways parents discipline children. Raising and training pets is very similar to raising and training children according to God's rules, and the child can learn this from his parents and his pets.

Discipline Proverbs

- "There are no gains without pains"(Benjamin Franklin, *Poor Richard's Almanac,* Bantam Books, 1976, p.4).

- Learn from the bee
  How to behave.
  Honeys for the good,
  Stings for the knave.

TEENAGE TEMPERING

18. Streets of San Francisco

As I look back, 1939 was a great year to live in San Francisco. The streets were filled with cable cars; the ferryboats still sailed; Alcatraz was legally occupied; and the World's Fair proclaimed the Depression was at an end.

We moved to the city so dad and mom could find work. Our apartment was on Hyde Street, where I caught the cable car for Marina Junior High School. I was now thirteen and old enough to be taught the art of shoplifting by an older classmate whom I shall call Roger.

Roger and I were walking home, having spent our cable car fares for candy. "Let's stop at the bakery on Van Ness," Roger suggested, "and pick up some French bread."

"That's a good idea," I agreed. Since arriving in San Francisco my addiction for French bread had become quite a habit.

We arrived at the bakery, and Roger guided me into a back alley. "You be the lookout, Jack," he ordered.

"Sure," I gushed in my innocence. "What do you want me to look out for?"

"Don't be funny!" growled Roger. "Just be sure to warn me if you see any cops."

Cops! It finally flashed in my country bumpkin of a brain that Roger was about to rob a bakery. I was horrified!

"You're going to steal some bread?" I asked in awe.

"You didn't think I was going to pay for it, did you?" he demanded.

"But suppose we get caught?" I argued, aware that Alcatraz had accommodations for those who broke the Eighth Commandment.

"We won't get caught, if you watch for the cops," Roger explained. "What's—a—matter, are you scared?"

"No!" I lied.

Roger slipped off and wormed through a back door while I tried to look out for everything. In a few seconds he came bursting back with a loaf under each arm.

"Run!" he yelled. I dashed after him down the alley and for the next four blocks. When we were satisfied that there was no pursuit, we sat on a curb to devour the wages of iniquity.

"Here's yours," Roger handed me a loaf. He took a bite. "Rats!" he exclaimed, "it's stale!" My bite confirmed the bitter truth and I chucked the bread into the gutter, following Roger's example.

"There's a real easy market on Polk Street," Roger mentioned. "We could get some candy there."

"Would I look out in the alley?" I asked.

"Naw, this time you come inside and look out for the clerks. Those guys are always on the prowl," Roger instructed.

"Clerks—I got it," I agreed.

"Just don't act suspicious," he warned, "or they'll grab you and start asking questions."

"Right," I repeated. "Don't act suspicious."

"If they ask ya what you're looking for, tell them Lucerne milk," Roger continued.

"Milk, I'm after milk," I echoed.

"Not milk, you dummy!" Roger roared, "Lucerne milk!"

"But why Lucerne milk?" I asked.

"Because they don't have any," Roger replied.

"That's silly," I objected. "Why would I be looking for something they don't have."

"Boy, are you stupid!" Roger said with disgust. "Only Safeway Stores have Lucerne milk. So when we tell them, then they'll tell us we have to go to a Safeway Store, and we can leave without any trouble."

My mind was spinning under all of Roger's instructions and explanations. Crime was certainly complicated.

Inside the store, I followed Roger down the aisles and observed his method of depositing candy bars in his pockets. He was about half loaded, when a clerk spotted his handiwork and yelled, "Hey, kid!"

"Beat it!" Roger hissed as he bolted for the door. Everything happened so fast that I stood frozen, immobilized by ignorance. Roger made good his escape while I was captured and hauled off to the manager's office.

"Boss," the clerk explained, "I saw these two kids swiping candy. The bigger one got away, but I caught this one."

"Not again," the boss sighed. "All right, kid, empty your pockets!"

I turned them inside out revealing a rubber band, pocketknife and a worn leather wallet.

"No candy," observed the boss.

"But he was with the bigger kid," insisted the clerk, "and I saw his buddy stealing candy."

"Were you with the other kid?" asked the boss.

"Yes, sir," I whispered.

"Did he swipe some candy?" the boss questioned.

"Yes, " I confessed.

"Do you want me to call the cops," he continued, "and let them take you home?"

The thought of facing my mother as a common thief, bringing her shame, terrified me after what she taught me from God's Word. For the first time in several years I experienced a bout with stuttering.

"P–P–P–Please," I pleaded, "d–d–d–don't call the cops."

The manager studied me over in silence. Satisfied that I was sincere, he let me go with a final warning. "I never want to see your face again!"

I gulped my gratitude, still too emotional to talk without stammering, and fled. My flight was straight for home, but Roger was waiting for me several blocks away.

"What did they do?" he demanded.

"Nothing," I answered, "they let me go."

"Did you tell them my name?" he questioned.

"Naw, I didn't tell them nothin'," I replied. Only when he was convinced that I had not squealed on him, did he offer me a candy bar. I refused.

"Go on," he persisted. "You earned it."

"I'm not hungry," I said.

Roger didn't press the matter. "Where ya going?" he asked.

"Home," I answered. "I've got work to do."

"Say, there's a dime store on Larkin," Roger remembered, "and they've got those big water guns. There's only one clerk, and she's old and crippled up. How 'bout it?"

Two strikes were enough for me. "I told you I had work to do at home," I said, firmly.

"Work?" Roger scoffed. "You ain't got no work, you're just plain yellow!"

"O.K., I'm yellow," I agreed.

Since we both agreed about my cowardice, there was nothing left to prove or argue over. We parted in complete agreement: Roger didn't want a Christian sissy for a partner; and I didn't want a thieving friend.

I went home and threw myself into a repentance of work. There were floors to mop, dishes to wash, and potatoes to peel. Roger failed in his attempts to instruct me in the way of robbery. Wholesome sweat from my daily chores just leached the sweetness out of stealing.

Discipline Principles

Children are influenced and guided by their peers, especially when these peers leaders are idolized and have more experience. But, years of childhood training in the Scriptures are not easily overcome, even by persistent peer pressure.

Parents who ignore, excuse, and justify wrong behavior in their children are insuring a harvest of heartaches.

Discipline Practices

Make an attempt to guide your child in selecting close friends. Weaker friendships may happen by chance, but it takes some effort to find and build good companions, particularly Christian friends.

Swift and immediate action has often deterred a budding life of crime. If a child's initial experiences with crime are successful, he'll probably continue in this course, especially if his friends are similarly engaged. Being caught at the beginning, and paying a small price, is far better than being caught at the end and facing the maximum sentence. Parents should be grateful when stores take a firm line against shoplifting, as this can help discourage further problems.

Discipline Proverbs

- "Wise men learn by others' harms; fools scarcely by their own" (Ben Franklin, *Poor Richard's Almanac*, Bantam Books, 1976, p.9).

- It takes a lot of courage to admit you're a coward.

- He who sleeps with the dogs wakes up with the fleas.

19. Sweet Slavery

"I've got this kid named, 'Good-game'," the coach quipped. "He's my fourth string quarterback." The students began to giggle. "Course, he's kind of a problem," the coach continued, "cause I only have enough players for three teams."

The students roared and I led the laughter. It was a real honor to be singled out by our coach at the pep rally for our big game with Red Bluff. I was living in Redding, California, and attended Shasta High School.

"Let me tell you about this Goodgame," the coach confided. "He's the smallest guy on the squad." I blushed as scores of eyes sought me out and sized me over. "But he's fast and sharp," the coach continued. "I mean really sharp. Last week against Weaverville they had a fast back called the Lizard. No one was tackling him, so I decided to send in Goodgame." The students leaned forward in happy anticipation.

"Goodgame goes in and the Lizard goes by. 'Get up!' I yells at Goodgame. So he gets up just in time to see the Lizard coming again. 'Get 'em!' I screams. Goodgame flies through the air for a shoestring tackle but the Lizard's wearing slippers and slips by. There's poor Goodgame, rolling in the grass. 'Get up!' I hollers, and he does. The Lizard reverses and heads back Goodgame's way. 'Get 'em high!' I warns Goodgame, but he misses again and just lays there in the grass, looking up at the sky. 'Goodgame!' I pleads, 'just don't lay there, get up and chase him!' You know what that Goodgame did? He just rolled over, looked at me, and said, 'Don't worry coach, he'll be back.' "

Playing football for Shasta High was a privilege. One evening, after a hard football practice, some of the players decided to go down to McColls for milkshakes.

"Coming, Goodgame?" asked King, our star tackle.

"Naw, I don't have the time," I answered. They looked sort of skeptical, so I added, "by the time I get home, eat supper, do my homework, and wash the dishes, it'll be time—"

I never finished the sentence. King roared, "Wash the *what?*"

"Wash the dishes," I repeated, "I always—"

King cut me off short. He took it upon himself to inform the entire team, to say nothing of innocent bystanders, of my household chores. "Hey, guys, get a load of this," King whooped. "Goodgame still washes the dishes!" This started a chain reaction of conversation.

"Bob, do you wash the dishes?" asked King.

"Never!" rejoiced Bob, who passed it on. "George do you wash the dishes?"

"Who, me?" laughed George. "I stopped that in the third grade! Fred, do you wash the dishes?" And so it went on until the entire team had publicly denied any association with washing dishes.

"Looks like you're the only one," gloated King.

"What's so bad about doing dishes?" I challenged.

"What's so bad?" King cried. "Didn't you ever read your history book?"

"History?" I questioned. "There's no dish-washing in history."

"Haven't you heard about Abraham Lincoln?" King retorted.

"What's Lincoln got to do with it?" I snapped.

"Why, Lincoln freed the slaves!" King roared.

Who was I to dispute President Lincoln? I left my buddies firmly determined that my dishwashing chains had been broken. The problem would be explaining my emancipation to mother.

After supper, I escaped to my studies and completed them in short order. When homework was over, I was allowed to listen to the radio, which I now did. I glued my ear to the speaker and was soon lost in "Jack Armstrong," "Gangbusters," and "The Green Hornet."

Mother found me at the radio, and said, "I've cleared the table and the dishes are in the sink."

I nodded but kept on listening. In a few minutes she was back. "Jack, it's getting late," she suggested. "You'd better get on those dishes."

There is just no way to say "No" tactfully to a persistent mother, and mine was no exception. I dreaded the crisis, but the fear of facing my football buddies acted as a catalyst to toughen my convictions.

"No," I said as meekly as I could.

"No?" mother questioned.

"No," I gathered up strength. "I'm not going to do the dishes."

"Are you sick?" mother asked with some concern .

"Yes!" I cried, sensing an opening. "I'm sick and tired of doing dishes!"

"Oh, I see," mother replied. "Are you also sick and tired of eating supper?"

"Of course not," I answered. "But I'm too big to wash dishes."

"Jack, let's get one thing straight," mother informed. "In this house if you don't work, then you don't eat. Dishes are your work, so get in there and do them."

It was a direct command. To disobey would be pure rebellion. I felt I was doomed, whatever the outcome, and in despair I blurted out my feelings.

"How come I have to wash dishes?" I cried. "There's not another boy on the football team that does them. I'm nothing around this house but a slave—a common slave, and Lincoln freed the slaves."

I had mother there, or at least I thought so. She was silent for a few moments and this gave me cause for hope.

"Well, I'm beginning to see your problem," she confessed. "You're tired of being a common slave."

"That's right!" I rejoiced. It was so good to have such an understanding mother.

"Fine," mother soothed. "You are no longer a common slave."

I sighed with utter relief, amazed at how simple it was to win my way.

"All right, *Royal Slave!*" mother thundered, "get into that kitchen and do those dishes, and I mean now!"

I jumped up from the radio in obedience to her authority before I realized what I had done. We stood there, and I tried to get a hurt look on my face, but the game was up. The thought of being a royal slave was too precious for silence, and we both started laughing—all the way to the kitchen.

Mother tied the apron around my waist, gave me a tender kiss, and left me to my duties. I was a bit unsure of exactly how a royal slave acted, so to be on the sure side, I did a royal job of washing the dishes. There was one consolation, I could honestly report to my teammates that I was no longer a common slave.

A few months later, when I had grown accustomed to my royal status, mother freed me completely. She made no big issue or display, she just did the dishes herself. I still did other work around the house for her, but doing dishes became history for me in more ways than one.

Discipline Principles

Teenagers face a difficult time during the process of cutting the apron strings of parental authority. Parents should not confuse their fledgling flights for independence as signs of defiance and rebellion. A sense of humor definitely helps to keep discipline situations under control and in proper perspective.

In reaching maturity, young people are influenced by many adults. Parents should not be resentful or jealous when their children receive help and guidance elsewhere.

Discipline Practices

As children grow older they will be under constant pressure from their peers to submit to group authority and control. Because children see life differently, there will be times of conflict between parental control and peer pressure. There are some basic concepts which can be of help during these upheavals.

Assurance. Assure the child that you do understand the situation, having endured the same when you were young. Talk over how grandfather and grandmother dealt with you, and how you reacted.

Compromise. Avoid as much as possible forcing the child to decide between you or the group. In these "either/or" dilemmas, both parents and children come out battered and bruised. There are ways to compromise and still maintain control.

Talking. Take time to talk things over with your child, calmly and patiently. The child must eventually leave home and stand alone, and his group of friends is a half-way house to full independence. Sooner or later, in the process of becoming adults, youth must break the bonds of peer pressure. Explain to your child that his friends will not always be with him to do his thinking, unless of course he happens to marry one of them. Help the child to understand that "slavery" to a group is just as distasteful as "slavery" to parents.

Acceptance. The child should understand that one does not have to obey and follow the group in all things to gain their acceptance. This can be proved by the scientific method of observation, and with a little guidance, your child will be able to realize this. You can wear a different style of shoes, not chew bubblegum, or even get "A's" at school, and still be accepted and respected by your friends.

Friendship. Discuss friends and what constitutes true friendship. The child through observing, talking, reading, and experience will discover what makes a friend. You can "hint" about a few good requirements:

- A true friend accepts you for what you are, not for what he can get out of you.

- Those who insist on thinking for you reveal their contempt for your mentality.

- Those who would rule over you are the ones you should rule out.

- A good friend stays by you, even when the going gets rough.

Peer pressure is another step on the search to maturity. It helps stimulate a child's thirst for responsible independence. Those who fail to break out of the protective shell of the group will always be vulnerable to the whims of others. The final issue is not whether the child will obey parents and peers; but whether the child will be able to discard these crutches and finally stand on his own two feet of self-discipline.

Discipline Proverbs

- Laughter lifts but ridicule ruins.

- Those who are willing to stand alone rarely need to do so.

- If you aren't willing to think for yourself, don't worry; there's a long line of people waiting to do it for you.

- The frustration of being a teenager, is that by the time you've figured out the answers, you've outgrown the problems.

- Discrimination is a one-way mind on a two-way street.

- "There is a friend that sticketh closer than a brother" (*Proverbs 18:24*).

20. Creosote Pole

The immediate effect of World War II on my teenage group was unlimited job opportunities. When I was fifteen dad arranged for my first man-sized work experience— construction of a dock at the Benecia Arsenal.

My simple task during the summer months was to paint creosote. Creosote is a chemical used on wood to discourage termites and worms. It is an acid that blisters, and on hot days the fumes reach out to search and sear. If you've never had a whiff of creosote, try sniffing a telephone pole on a hot day.

I scampered over the dock, as it was being built, and smeared creosote on exposed timbers. My equipment was a five gallon pail and a long handled brush. The work was hellish, both from the burning brew I sloshed about, and the danger of working high above the bay balanced on a six-inch timber. The liquid was so caustic that the soles on two pairs of boots were literally eaten away. Both my hands and face peeled several times before my skin was callous enough to defend itself. Of the creosote painting crew, I was the only boy who lasted the entire summer. Ten hours a day, seven days a week, didn't allow much time for this juvenile to become delinquent.

"Where's your card?" a union steward asked me one day. I gave him my union card, which he checked over.

"This is a laborer's card," he growled. "You can't paint creosote. That's pile–butt work!"

He ordered me off the dock, and I headed back to the office shack to see what new assignment my boss would give me. The thought of leaving creosote to the pile–butts was perfectly fine with me. I entered the shack.

"What's the matter, Jack?" he asked.

"I can't paint creosote anymore," I replied.

"You're not quitting, are you?" the boss questioned.

I explained that the union steward had run me off the job and that I could only do laborer's work. My boss listened, then marched me back to the dock and the unjust steward.

"You won't let this man paint creosote?" he asked.

"That's right," the steward answered. "He's not a pile–butt, and the regulations state that—"

"O.K., O.K.," the boss cut him off. "I know the regulations. You're a pile–butt, so from now on *you* paint the creosote."

"Not me!" the steward replied in great indignation. "I'm the job steward."

"In that case," ordered the boss, "you assign someone to do the painting. I'm going to be back in five minutes and somebody better be swabbing. Because if nobody is, you better, and if you won't, you're fired! Understand?"

I stood there with my bucket and brush, not knowing how I could avoid a union civil war. The steward was in a sweat. He certainly wasn't going to paint creosote, but neither did he dare order one of the pile-butts to do so. His only way out was to swallow his pride, forget the regulations, and order me to do it.

"All right, kid," he tried to sound gruff, "I'll let you off this time. Get to work."

The next couple of weeks the steward was on my back. No matter how hard I worked, he found cause for complaints and plastered me with them. One day he was boring holes out on the end of the dock and needed some creosote. He yelled for me to come. I had to walk on the top of a six-inch timber some thirty feet above the water, and he wasn't too impressed with my caution.

"Hurry up!" he ordered. "I ain't got all day."

When I reached his position he grabbed the bucket and swabbed the hole and timber. "How can we get this job done," he grumbled, "using kids to do men's work?" I knew better than to answer. He handed the bucket back to me, slipped a washer over the bolt, and rammed it down the hole. It was a reckless move, motivated by anger and impatience. He paid dearly for it. The bolt slammed home; the washer hit the timber and threw creosote in all directions. I was standing and the splash went clear up to my waist, but the steward was kneeling and took it full in the face.

Painful profanity is about the best description I can give to his initial expressions. I backed away from the enraged beast while he cursed the entire creation.

"It's all your fault!" he roared. "If you hadn't been so slow!"

The only thing that saved me was his blinded condition, otherwise I'm certain he would have chased me to Vallejo for revenge. His cursing quickly attracted attention, and the other pile-butts came to his rescue. They helped him back to the main portion of the dock, where an ambulance rushed him to the hospital. I later heard that his blindness was only temporary, but I never saw him on the dock again.

The creosote worked through my pants and started on my legs. I had to find another set of pants, and take a shower, to avoid some painful blisters. It was all in a day's job as I worked at becoming a man.

Discipline Principles

Maturity is a process that requires association. Little boys long to be around the bigger boys and imitate them. Through this companionship they develop into youth. Young people need experiences with adults to guide them into full adulthood. By "beholding" we "are changed" is a law of life for the physical and spiritual natures of man (see *2 Corinthians 3:18*).

Many of the problems teenagers attract could be avoided if they were kept occupied in productive employment.

Discipline Practices

There are many advantages in training our children to respect and engage in honest work.

Work enhances self-respect. A job well done, regardless of the wages earned, is its own reward. Pride in workmanship, in doing the best job possible, makes any work worthwhile. Solomon expressed this philosophy of life in these words: "And also that every man should eat and drink, and enjoy the good of all his labour, it is the gift of God" (*Ecclesiastes 3:13*).

Work precludes indiscretions. A busy boy simply doesn't have the time to fool around, and a tired boy doesn't have the energy. Children if left to themselves too long will invent devices for mischief. Jesus knew the importance of keeping busy, and He commanded His disciples to "Occupy till I come" (*Luke 19:13*).

Work is healthful. "The man who works hard sleeps well whether he eats little or much, but the rich must worry and suffer insomnia" (*Ecclesiastes 5:12, LB*).

A boy should have samples of doing a man's job, but it should not be his steady diet. Constant pressure ages a person before his time.

All work and no play,
Makes Jack a man before his day.
The opposite is just as wild,
Poor Jack will always be a child.

It is enough that a boy attempts to do a man's job, even if he fails to complete it. Success comes with experience.

Discipline Proverbs

- Labor leaves little for the imagination to indulge.

- To sow in anger is to reap in strife.

- All the wealth of welfare cannot buy one ounce of independence.

21. Black Magi

The summer of '43 Dad landed me a job on Mare Island Naval Yard as a carpenter's helper. This was a definite promotion from painting creosote. I had worked a couple of weeks when the boss took me aside.

"How'd you like to earn more money?" he asked.

"Not if it's painting creosote," I answered, fearing that my reputation had followed me.

"No, it's working on a section gang," he explained. "They're short a man and need a good worker."

I felt a pang of pride at being considered a good worker, but was suspicious over any job that paid more money. "What's a section gang?" I questioned.

"You'll be laying railroad track in the ammunition dump," he answered.

That explained the extra pay—working around live ammunition was slightly dangerous. I agreed. He drove me to my new job and introduced me to the new boss.

"Deacon, here's your new hand," was all he said, and left.

Deacon was an elderly Negro who had come

out of retirement to help in the war effort. He quickly looked me over.

"You work on a gang before?" he asked.

"No, sir." I could see that he was more than slightly disappointed, and I began to feel like an outcast. My former boss had failed to inform me that I would be the only white on an all black crew. Being white was bad enough under those conditions, but being green as well was horrible.

"Let me see those hands," Deacon demanded.

I showed my hands and he looked them over. For the first time I noted a sign of respect as he viewed the evidence of hard labor—plenty of calluses.

"Give the boy a hammer," Deacon ordered.

A hammer was slapped into my hand, and I couldn't believe it was for real. I knew a little about hammers, even sledges, but what they gave me was ridiculous! The handle was too short, and both heads were too long. The tool had the appearance of a squashed capital letter "T". At first I suspected they were giving me the railroad version of the "left handed monkey wrench."

"Now watch me," Deacon ordered. He took his hammer, and with a partner began driving spikes. Their harmony of hammering won my instant admiration.

"You try it," Deacon commanded.

For the next fifteen minutes I provided the entertainment for the entire section gang. I displayed a talent for hitting the rail, tie plate, tie, even the gravel; but hitting the spike eluded me.

"Ain't no man dare to work with you spiking," was Deacon's evaluation of my efforts. "Give 'em a bar."

A bar was thrust at me. It was six feet long,

about an inch thick, and consisted of solid steel. One end was pointed like a spear, the other squared off like a bar of soap. Deacon explained the purpose of this instrument.

"The train runs on the rails, the rails on the ties, and the ties on the gravel. With this here bar we knocks the gravel under the ties and packs it in tight. You understand?"

I watched as Deacon and his partner worked down both sides of a tie, ramming and tamping the gravel firmly underneath. By now I was beginning to suspect that everything done on a section gang was done in pairs. I wondered how Deacon would pair me off, and glanced at the other men.

"You try it," Deacon said, and he handed me his bar. I was shocked at its weight. With his partner, I tamped away, and tried to keep up. It was necessary that we work directly opposite each other, otherwise we'd drive the gravel clear under the tie and out the other side.

"He might make a tamper," Deacon suggested. "You work with him, Fred."

"Why me?" cried Fred in obvious dismay.

"Cause I told you to!" Deacon answered.

I sensed that Fred was probably being punished for some past dereliction or disrespect. He appeared to be in his early twenties. The gang swung into action, and I followed Fred to our place of labor.

Fred went to work; I mean he really poured it on! I was forced to use every muscle and grit of determination to keep up. Every tie was a race, as we rammed our way across the tracks. It didn't take long for this unusual work style to play havoc with my arms. My muscles weren't used to this type of exercise, and both arms soon felt like dead lead.

I became suspicious of Fred's pace. He seemed dedicated to the proposition that if he worked me into the ground, I'd quit. I felt the entire gang was in on this plot, since no one bothered to talk to me.

During the water break I reviewed my predicament. Fred was larger and stronger, to say nothing of his skill, so keeping up with him was going to be a ball of wasps. I was convinced that my arms could not last the day unless they received some backup support. Fatigue forced me to invent a new technique for tamping.

Ramming the bar was fairly easy, since gravity lent a hand. It was the lifting that tuckered me out. I started lifting with my body, all of it: feet, ankles, legs, lungs—whatever was available. This relieved the strain on my arms, but it gave me the appearance of doing ballet tippy–toes. Fred was clearly embarrassed by my unorthodox tamping and tried to leave me behind, but I hung on. When the whistle blew, I dropped the bar and walked off without speaking or being spoken to.

That night, mother used horse liniment to resurrect what remained of my arm muscles. I went to bed early, exhausted. The next morning I ate mostly oatmeal, which I knew would stick to my ribs and hold me until lunch. The gang seemed surprised at my return, and Fred looked glum. It was another hard day's work, with no mercy asked or given. The rest of the crew kept up a constant flow of laughter and chatter, but Fred and I suffered in silence.

By the third day my body was feeling back to normal, as muscles regrouped and adjusted themselves. I was working along at the usual rapid rate, head down and pounding, when to my surprise I beat Fred to the end of the tie.

"Boy," growled Fred, "you trying to make me look bad?"

I didn't appreciate being falsely accused or referred to as a "boy." It was with double delight that I got some hot chestnuts off my mind. "You're the one that's trying to show off," I challenged. "But if you think you can work me off this job, you're nuts!"

Fred raised his bar and I considered the possibility of having him twist it around my big mouth. I made some mental preparations for a fast flight down the tracks. Our sudden outburst caused the Deacon to hasten over.

"What's all this?" he demanded.

Fred gave his version first. I followed with my rendition which agreed with his in interest but not in principle. The Deacon listened carefully, then gave his verdict. I was now given my first lesson in section gang protocol.

"Don't you never beat a man like that again!' he ordered. "Not on my gang, not on anybody's gang. You hear!"

"How did I know Fred was going to quit early?" I protested.

"We all works at the same speed," Deacon continued. "I sets the pace and you all follows. I know Fred worked you good and proper, but he was just testing you. You want to be on this gang, then you don't go running off on the job."

The thought of slowing down to a civilized race cooled my anger. "Yes, Mr. Deacon," I rejoiced, "I'll be happy to slow down. But I still don't like being called 'boy' when I'm doing a man's job."

"Fair enough," he approved. "What's your name?"

"Jack."

"Then, Jack it is," concluded the Deacon. Thereafter, the others addressed me as "Jack" or "man" which indicated I had been accepted as a member of the gang. I was still not a friend, or even a close facsimile of one. I didn't push, knowing my place, and they didn't pull. It was the Deacon who finally extended the right hand of friendship during a lunch break.

"Jack," he called, "you want to swap sandwiches?"

"Sure," I replied, happy for this invitation to be a part of the group. I hurried over from my lonely position and gave him the first choice. He rummaged through my pail, then settled for a chicken salad. It was my turn to select, and I checked his rations. Not wanting to give the impression that I was too good for his food, I took the top sandwich. It was the Deacon's privilege to bite first.

"Not bad, for chicken," he mumbled with a mouthful.

They all watched as I navigated my mouth about the Deacon's specialty. I crunched down and ended up confused. There was nothing in my past, present, or future to define what I had dug into.

"Like it?" Deacon purred.

"It's different," I cried without thinking, then hastily added, "What I mean is that it's good and different!"

"Ought to be," chuckled the Deacon. "Know what it is?"

"Not for sure," I honestly replied.

"It's blackeyed peas, mustard greens, and fatback!" roared the Deacon. At his revelation, the saints came bursting in on a cloud of laughter. Since all the crew were smiling and grinning, I took it as a family joke and laughed right back on them. Besides, it really didn't taste all that bad, now that I knew what it was. With a no—nonsense, down—to—earth, blackeyed pea sandwich our friendship began.

In a few days I felt secure enough to return the compliment. I had mother make some good, old-fashioned Polish bread with a crust thick enough to be respectable. She also whipped up a Slavic specialty which I knew would bewilder the Deacon.

"Deacon, would you like to swap sandwiches?" I invited.

"Wouldn't mind if I did," he accepted with a grin. The crew clustered around, sensing the birth of a prank. Deacon was a good sport and took the top sandwich, but it really didn't matter, as all my sandwiches were the same. As before, he had the right of the first bite.

"Like it?" I teased.

"That sure is good bread," he volunteered.

"Sure ought to be," I proclaimed. "My mother made it from a Polish recipe. Know what's inside?"

"No," the Deacon confessed, "I can't quite lay my tongue on it."

"It's Polish *kapusta!*" I howled. At the sound of *kapusta*, Deacon stopped chewing. He just held the load in his jaws, ashamed to spit and afraid to swallow.

"Ka . . . what?" laughed Fred, who relished seeing the Deacon all choked up.

"*Kapusta*," I cried. "That's Polish cabbage!"

The mention of "cabbage" had a medicinal effect on the Deacon, and he swallowed with a sigh of relief. "Jack," he questioned, "that sure don't taste like cabbage to me."

"Oh, yes, it is!" I insisted. "Fresh out of our garden. Only we don't hack it into sauerkraut like those stupid Germans." (Let me apologize to all sauerkraut lovers for this uncouth remark of my younger days. You must remember that during this war time the Germans were the enemy.)

"What's it taste like?" Fred asked. I gave him a sandwich and he tore into it. "What did your momma do to that cabbage?" he cried.

"Haven't you got any taste at all?" I hedged.

"Got me stumped," Fred gulped. "First it's sweet, next it's sour. That cabbage can't make up its mind."

With pride and pleasure I then described the magic of making *kapusta*. Fred was correct in his confusion, for it's a sweet–sour entree, brewed to a gourmet's delight. The good Deacon ate the entire sandwich and then gave his blessing.

"Jack, if we mixed up a batch of your *kapusta* with a mess of our blackeyed peas," he paused, savoring the combination, "man! we'd have something really good!" The laughter that followed was just that.

Good food led to good conversation. Not that we always agreed, for neither my black friends nor I had to stoop to condescension.

On a hot afternoon, Fred laid slavery on my soul. "You people made slaves out of us," he pronounced.

I stopped tamping and faced him squarely. "Then how come I'm not boss of this gang?" I countered.

He fretted over my answer and went back to tamping before coming up with a reply. "What I meant was, that your people come over to Africa and stole us to America."

"Fred," I lectured, "all of my people were in Poland when that happened. Why, my grandparents didn't come to this country until way after the Civil War!"

That took the joy out of Fred's contentions for the afternoon.

On another occasion, during lunch, we got to arguing as to who had been the poorest. Fred gave a graphic description of the squalor he had been forced to survive in. It was then my turn to explain what real poverty was all about.

"You don't even know what hard times are," I scoffed. "When I was a child, we moved to Florida, and had to live with the poor–white–trash. We were so poor that my folks couldn't send me to school!"

Fred was impressed by my claiming to have lived in the South and not having attended school, but he wasn't about to heave in the towel. "What I hear," he persisted, "that down in the South, even the white–trash look down on us!"

"That's right!" chorused some of the crew who had lived in Dixie.

"You didn't let me finish," I objected. "We weren't just any common ordinary white–trash. We were Northern Polack poor–white–trash! The only thing a Southerner hates more than a Yankee is a Polack Yankee. Why, no decent white–trash kids would even think to play with me. I had to cross over the railroad tracks and play with the colored kids. That's how poor I was!"

Fred sat speechless, stunned by my portrayal of Polish poverty. "Are you funnin' me?" was about all he could reply.

"No, it just could be true," the Deacon interjected in my behalf. "Something about Jack tells me he's been around our people before."

It would be wrong to leave the impression that I always won these verbal contests. More than once the Deacon taught me what true intelligence is all about.

Fred and I were engaged in our favorite topic of conversation over the relative merits of Blacks and Poles. "Just name me one famous Polish king," Fred requested. I tried, but my knowledge of Polish nobility wasn't worth repeating.

"Ain't got no Polish king! Ain't got no Polish king!" Fred sang and tamped his bar in rhythm.

"If you're so smart, name me one of your African kings," I countered.

"Pharaoh!" cried Fred, and then started to sing. "We got Pharaoh away down in Egypt land."

"Pharaoh?" I gasped. "Why, he was a white man!"

"He was?" Fred asked.

"Sure he was," I insisted. "Egypt's way up in the north."

"Well, I do believe you're right," Fred mocked, "because no black king would–a made slaves out of God's people!"

Fred didn't trap me too often, but when he did, it was inexcusable. I kept up my attack. "Come on, now, name me a black African king."

Fred thought and considered, but it was now his turn to burn from ignorance. I couldn't resist the chance to goad. "You can't come up with one out of a whole continent? They must have all been slaves!"

"Watch your mouth," Fred cautioned, "unless you can do better."

"Oh, I can," I boasted, "at least I know an African king."

"You foolin' me?" Fred warned.

"No, honest," I answered. "There was this

great big guy down in southern Africa I read about."

"What's his name?" Fred demanded, somewhat hopefully.

"Let's see," I pondered. "They named Africa after him. It was Afrikaner. Because he was so great, that's how Africa got its name." Fred really brightened at this piece of misinformation.

"Afrikaner—" Fred mused, "uh, uh, I likes that name!"

"Well, not many did," I explained. "He was one mean man."

"Mean, too?" Fred cried with happiness.

"Not only mean, he was ugly!" I continued. "Even the sight of him was enough to cause most people to shut their eyes. His armies whipped everybody, including the white guys. And you asked me if he was mean?"

"Mercy!" sighed a contented Fred. "But don't stop now, what else happened?"

"Let's see," I paused to recollect dusty memories. "He finally got so bad that they sent off to England for a doctor."

"A doctor?" Fred snapped. "Why a doctor?"

"Guess they figured he had the medicine to tame him," I replied, putting the cheese on the trap.

Fred sniffed suspiciously and edged in closer. "You making all this up?"

"Fred!" I wailed in hypocrisy, "I wouldn't fool around with something as serious as this. I even remember the doctor they sent for. You've heard of Dr. David Livingstone?"

"Yeah, I know him," Fred said. "But what did they want to tame Afrikaner for anyway?"

"They had to do something," I soothed. "You can't let a man loose who is stealing and burning and killing all over the place. So they brought down Livingstone cause he had the medicine to tame him."

Fred nibbled the bait. "How'd they do that?"

"No problem, Doc Livingstone made a white man out of him!" I roared.

"Deacon!" Fred bawled, "Jack's making fun of us again, and I'm getting a mad on!"

The Deacon trudged over to settle the dust. "When you boys going to grow up?" he inquired.

"Was there this black king called Afrikaner?" Fred asked.

"That's right," the faithful Deacon replied.

"There was?" poor Fred exclaimed. "Then why'd he let them make a white man out of him?"

"Jack was just teasing," Deacon answered. "What happened was that Afrikaner became a Christian."

"See, Fred!" I butted in. "I told you so."

"You messed up the story some," Deacon corrected. "It was a Mr. Moffat, not Dr. Livingstone, who helped Afrikaner."

"You're probably right," I conceded, "but at least I knew more about black kings than Fred did." Fred glared, but kept silent.

"Sounds like you do a lot of reading," spoke the Deacon. "Ever read the Bible?"

"Sure," I boasted. "I read it all the time."

"That's good," Deacon praised. "Mind if I ask a question to check on all that reading?"

"Ask away," I invited.

"Where was it in the Bible," the Deacon quizzed, "that when the rooster crowed, all the world heard it?"

It was too easy, and I surmised trickery. Fred,

hopefully, looked for my ignorance.

"Well," the Deacon prodded, "does you know?"

"Everybody knows that one," I derided. "The rooster crowed three times to let the whole world know that Peter had betrayed Jesus."

"That's strange," Deacon sighed. "I always thought it was Judas that betrayed Jesus."

"Judas did it. Judas did it!" yelled Fred, remembering his Sunday school lessons.

I had been tripped on a technicality! Deacon had given me such a simple question, that I blew it. "Yeah, you're right," I agreed. "Judas betrayed and Peter denied. But it was still that rooster."

"You mean to tell me," Deacon inquired, "they heard that rooster clear to China?"

"Huh?" was about all I could confess as the Deacon's logic laid me low. I'd been had. I knew it, the Deacon knew it, and worst of all, Fred knew it!

"Give up?" Deacon asked.

It was physically impossible for any rooster to be heard round the world. "O.K." I whimpered, "what's the joke?"

"No joke," Deacon laughed. "He was the only rooster left, so he let the whole world know he was still alive."

"The only rooster left? That's impossible!" I protested.

"Not on Noah's Ark," was the Deacon's sweet reply.

"He gotcha! Deacon done gotcha!" Fred shouted for all to hear.

"He pulled a riddle on me," I argued. "Now that I know what to expect, it'll be different. You beat me on the Bible. How about trying something else?" I knew the Deacon hadn't gone to high school, so I figured I could take him on a secular subject.

"You much in arithmetic?" Deacon asked. "Can you add and take away?"

"I'm great in math," I replied, adding, "and I can also multiply and divide." I didn't mention my knowledge of algebra, figuring that might scare the Deacon into another topic.

"Get a pencil and paper, and write this problem down," the Deacon suggested. Fred and I rounded up the equipment. As the Deacon dictated, the entire crew listened.

"You have $100.00 to buy chickens with, and I wants you to spend exactly $100.00, not a cent more or less."

"I spend exactly $100.00," I repeated.

"I wants you to buy 100 chickens," the Deacon proceeded, "exactly 100 chickens with the $100.00. Now there's three kinds of chickens I want you to buy. Baby chicks, hens, and roosters."

"Baby chicks, hens, and roosters," I spoke as I wrote.

"Chicks cost a nickel, roosters a dollar, and hens are five dollars," he instructed. "Now I don't care how many of each, but I wants some of all kinds. So, spend $100.00 and buy 100 chickens and be sure to have some chicks, roosters, and hens."

"Is that all?" I asked.

"That's it," the Deacon concluded. "I'll give you three days to get the answer."

"Three days!" I scoffed. "I'll have it for you in the morning."

"No, take the three days," Deacon insisted. "I don't want you to lose too much sleep."

After supper, I started on the problem. After

several false starts, I decided to wrap it up quickly with my algebra know-how. I tried to work up an equation, but there were too many "unknowns" to contend with. At midnight, in disgust, I crept into bed.

Fred was on me first thing in the morning. "Got those chickens?" he asked.

"I was too tired last night," I said, "but tonight I'm going to figure it out."

My second night of ciphering proved as fruitless as the first. I was often close to the solution, but always it seemed I was a bird shy or a dollar high.

"How's them chickens?" Fred cackled the next morning.

"We had company last night," I said.

"Yeah, I bet," Fred said, somewhat slyly.

"Deacon gave me three days," I reminded my tormentor, "and I'll have it for sure, tomorrow."

The third night on Deacon's enigma proved the most frustrating of all. I used up sheets of paper and burned lead in my pencil until the wee hours of the morning. But as the wise man said, "All is vanity and vexation of spirit" (*Ecclesiastes 1:14*). My only hope was that the Deacon had tossed me a ringer.

When I arrived at work, Fred jumped me. "Got it?" he asked.

"Got what?" I retorted.

"You know, the chickens," he cried.

"Yeah," I replied. "I figured it out."

Fred looked downright disappointed. "Here comes the Deacon," he warned.

"Morning, Jack," Deacon greeted. "How are the chickens?"

"I got the answer," I said, somewhat hopefully.

"Fine, fine," he replied. "What is it?"

"The answer is," I paused, drew a breath, and

blurted, "there is no answer! It's an impossible problem like squaring the circle."

"No, Jack, you're wrong," Deacon spoke. "There's an answer."

"Do you know it?" I asked.

"I sure do," the Deacon grinned, "want me to tell you?"

"Oh, no!" I objected. "If there's an answer, I'll figure it out for myself."

It took three more days of trial and terror before I stumbled onto the secret. The minute Deacon saw my face, he knew I had it. "You got it?" he asked, already knowing my response.

"Yes, sir," I proclaimed, "and no one helped me."

"Then what is it?" Fred demanded. I started to answer but the Deacon hushed me. "Don't give this away free," he cautioned. "You just whisper it in my ear." Fred looked sheepish at being excluded.

"You sure did!" Deacon praised. "That's exactly it!"

"How do I know he done it?" cried Fred.

"Jack knows, and I knows, and that's all who needs to know," the Deacon chuckled.

For the next few days, Fred hounded and pleaded for the answer. I knew he was in real sincerity when he even offered to buy the truth from me. "Fred," I pontificated, "don't you know there are some things that money can't buy?"

The summer drew to a close and I was tempted to quit high school and stay with my section gang. The money was good and the company was even better. Fred, notwithstanding all his funning, sincerely hoped I'd stay. "You're not much," he teased, "but the next guy will be even worse." I finally asked the Deacon what he thought I ought to do.

"Jack," he answered, "best you make up your own mind, cause that's what a man's got to do. Just remember, long as I'm bossing, you got a place on my gang."

I decided to return to school, for my desire to learn outweighed the drive to earn. At the end of my last day on the gang, all of the crew came by to shake my hand and wish me well. Fred gave me a real knuckle buster straight from his heart. "Better brush up on that math," he teased as we squeezed hands. Deacon was the last to say good-bye.

"Jack, it's been good having you on the gang," he softly said.

"I'm glad I could work for you," I replied.

"I want you to know," Deacon continued, "that I'm truly proud you're going back to school. Don't let nobody keep you from that education, you hear?"

"Yes, sir," I agreed.

"I'm proud to lay a straight track, it's good work," Deacon went on with his wisdom. "But you'd make me prouder if you did something better with your mind, and made something out of yourself."

"I'll try," I promised.

"Just always remember," he finalized, "if you ain't your own man, then you're always going to be someone else's boy. I won't forget you, Jack, no not never."

Deacon's warmth and sincerity aroused my Polish emotions, and I struggled to hold back the tears. He must have sensed my feelings, for he pulled me to him, and gave me a good hug. Hugs I understood, and could return without choking over words.

Discipline Principles

When you can think for yourself, act for yourself, and accept full responsibility for being yourself, then you are yourself.

It is not a question whether the knowledge we gain is good, bad, or indifferent. The fact remains that we cannot avoid learning from others.

The prerequisite for becoming part of a group is that the group becomes part of you. There is a natural inclination for children and adults to join a group. We desire to belong and become like others, even if this means submission to group rules and regulations. There is also a survival instinct that unity with others satisfies. Solomon described it in these words: "Two are better than one; because they have a good reward for their labour. For if they fall, the one will lift up his fellow: but woe to him that is alone when he falleth; for he hath not another to help him up" (*Ecclesiastes 4:9, 10*).

Discipline Practices

There are a few basic points to remember and practice which will increase your chances for being accepted by a group.

Be yourself. Hypocrisy is a weak foundation on which to build a lasting and meaningful relationship.

Be patient. It takes time to earn respect and to be accepted by others. Being too pushy at the beginning usually insures being held off at arm's length. Give others a chance to see your finer points of character and then they'll be more inclined to excuse your rough edges.

Be friendly. "A man that hath friends must shew himself friendly ... " (*Proverbs 18:24*).

Be content. Avoid the temptation to find fault, change things, and begin an improvement program. People seek leaders, but they flee from judges.

We should desire and seek for deeper insights concerning people and their problems; but don't be blinded by your insights. The old Negro spiritual, "Nobody knows the trouble I've seen . . . " is as true today as when it was sung under slavery.

A visit to a prison and even living in a cell for awhile will certainly give new insights as to prison life; but visitation is not identical with incarceration. Wearing beads, running barefoot, and camping in the hills may open up new aspects of hippy–style life; but sampling is not the same as surviving. Realizing that you can leave a situation makes staying in it tolerable. Starvation and dieting are both predicated on not eating, but very few confuse the two as being identical.

Discipline Proverbs

- If you hurts my feelings, you're going to end up feeling my hurts.

- You incriminate yourself when you discriminate others.

- What you hear, you forget; what you see, you recall; but what you do, you know.

- Sour grapes don't get squeezed and pouting lips are rarely pleased.

- Don't judge a man until you've walked in his shoes for a month; however, never forget that you can always step out of his shoes.

- "Judge not . . . " (*Matthew 7:1*).

APPENDIX A

Specifications for Spanking

Never spank in anger. Parents must be in control of their emotions and muscles when physically punishing their children. Far better to delay and cool one's ardor than to immediately thrash in wrath.

Never spank in joy. The dispensing of pain is not a happy occasion for either parent or child. To express pleasure in punishing one's child is the lowest form of sadism.

Never injure the child. The pain produced by paddling should be temporary in time and limited in location. Society should not coddle or excuse those parental perverts who abuse and injure their children. Their punishment should be swift and sure, including the placement of their children in a proper home. To avoid injury and possible disfigurement:

- Only spank those areas of the body which can absorb pain without danger of permanent injury, such as the back, buttocks, and thighs. Areas that should never be struck are any part of the head, neck, fingers, and other joints.

- Use a proper instrument. A flexible object like a leather belt or willow switch will sting but not inflict deep bruises. A solid rigid object like a paddle or stick must be used with care to avoid injury. Do not strike too hard, too often, and close to the bones.

- Use discretion in the amount of force used in relationship to the size and physical condition of the child.

- Limit the number of swats, making them few but meaningful. Gentle love taps should not be offered as a substitute for a spanking. This practice only cheapens the parent and his punishment in the child's mind. Anything worth doing, including spanking, is worth doing well; for one effective spanking will preclude a host of feeble ones.

- While paddling is permissible, boxing ears, kicking, pulling hair, striking with the fist, and so forth, are not.

Never rush into spanking. Paddling should only be attempted after other more effective methods have been tried. The ancient proverb, "haste maketh waste," is especially applicable to spanking. Paddling should not be the entree on your menu of discipline, but rather the dessert.

The need for paddling decreases with age. Smaller children require constant physical attention and correction. Even an infant will learn to respond to a gentle tap on the arm accompanied by a firm, "no, no." But as a child grows, the need for physical correction diminishes and the desire to talk and reason increases. Rarely should older children be spanked, not only because they deeply resent such discipline, but also because there are more effective methods available.

Paddling should not be a constant threat. Do not harangue your child that you plan to spank him unless he changes his activities. This perpetual promise to punish, delayed and neglected, is of no effect. Be consistent. Speak once about spanking, and if ignored, then follow through with this commitment.

Counsel before spanking. A few choice words, and be careful how you select them, should precede this punishment. It is well worth your time to talk things over on a parent-to-child basis, and to explain:

- Why a spanking is necessary. Review briefly the other methods you attempted to correct the situation.

- The number of swats that will be administered. Avoid argument on this point, but keep the number small and reasonable, so that the child can see mercy mingled with justice.

- Express your love for the child, but displeasure in his misconduct.

- God loves the sinner, but hates the sin.

Parents should be united. It is better when both parents are willing and able to share the responsibility of correction. Parents should stand firmly together, and not allow their children to divide and play their sympathies against each other. When father is finally forced to punish, then mother should clearly support this discipline.

Follow up spankings with reconciliation. The purpose of spanking is to improve and not merely remove improper behavior. It is *after* the paddling that the iron is hot and amenable to shaping. Pain, even among adults, clears minds and awakens the senses. While the memory is still fresh, important lessons can be taught, and the child can understand the relationship between cause and effect. Whatever the problem, once the child is punished, he should be accepted with open arms with no strings attached. Under no provocation should the child be rejected and disowned.

Love must be expressed in spanking. Spanking, like other tribulations, will either draw us closer together or drive us farther apart. Properly applied, your child will see your love despite the pain.